THE FLESH OF THE SEA

LOR GISLASON

SHELLEY LAVIGNE

To all those still searching for their crew

Contents

Content Warning

The THRILLING and ENLIGHTENING
Accompte
of WILFORD BOWEN's
Adventures and Discoveries

Including Encounters with *Many Wondrous Creatures*
Heretofore Unknown to Science
WHILE SAILING TO THE
CARIBBEAN

with *Notes* and *Commentary*
BY HIS FRIEND
Jean Baptiste de Beaupré

June 17th, 1760

LETTER FROM WILFORD BOWEN TO JEAN BAPTISTE DE BEAUPRÉ

DEAREST JEAN BAPTISTE,

Don't be mad.

I've never seen you mad, so that might be a silly thing to say but when you read the rest of this letter, I imagine your smooth brow will crease and your steady hands will shake.

You always did think me a bit impulsive and rash, and this will no doubt reinforce those beliefs.

I'm stalling. I am having a hard time getting the words out. I won't tell you how many times I've rewritten this letter, but paper is precious and I need to conserve what I have.

You've probably already heard the news. I was denied a Royal Society Fellowship. I have no doubt that Peter has already stopped by to share this information. He is quicker than any postman will ever be, especially where Society business is concerned. I was quite happy that I could rely on him to tell you, not because I was embarrassed I wouldn't sit in the hallowed halls you already occupy, but rather because I couldn't bear to see your unsure, hesitant pity when you heard. I did not want to see you pinch your lips as you thought about where to lay your hand in comfort.

~~Especially after what happened last time we saw one another.~~

I do not need it, dear chum.

No, that was the push I needed.

The Society said I was not treading new ground, that my research on snail shells was entirely too similar to Dezalier d'Argenville's. They were right, I said nothing that had not been put more eloquently by others who have come before me.

But their words got me thinking. We hear more and more about lands east of the Atlantic. So many new places, so many new things to see. So I took the train to Bristol to find employment or passage on one of the Navy ships. Apparently, a man versed in Latin and anatomy (even if I know my way around a snail better than I do a human being) is in high demand as a doctor. My Captain welcomed me aboard enthusiastically; the last chap had never even cut into any living thing and fainted dead away at the first sight of blood.

I've never left England, while you've at least seen France. I've seen no great wonders, ~~except for you my dear friend~~. I've always just dreamed of the world beyond our borders. Well, I'd like to see it with my eyes, touch things I can't even imagine!

We learn not for life but for school, our Professor once said, remember? *Non vitae sed scholae.* Well, I think it's about time I did the opposite.

Maybe then, I'll come back with the greatest discoveries the Royal Society has ever seen, and we can continue to sit side by side, just as we've done since Oxford. I would like that very much. I would like to prove to ~~you~~ them my value, make it impossible for them to turn me away.

And this has nothing to do with that drunken night, I promise. I know you say you don't recall what happened, and I wanted to tell you before going away, but I cannot put the words to paper. I don't want you to think that I'm running away because of you, or that I am angry.

I am doing this for me.

I will post this now because we are leaving soon. There are

rumours of pirates off the coast and we want to make it to open water and stay clear. I will send you news when I can.

~~Yours,~~
~~Best wishes,~~
Yours,
Wilford Bowen

June 19th, 1760

ENTRY FROM JEAN BAPTISTE DE BEAUPRÉ'S JOURNAL

I CANNOT SAY I'm particularly surprised by Wilford's actions, but I am still saddened he did not call on me before he left. Say his good-byes. I wouldn't have been able to talk him out of his foolish venture —he's always been much too wilful (perhaps cursed by his name) to listen to my counsel—but I would have welcomed the opportunity to try.

Or the chance to see his face again.

I'd hate for the last image I have of him to be that of his distant, slouching figure walking away from his Royal Society interview. The weight of his sadness had pressed down on my shoulders and I'd wished we could have carried it together, if only he'd let me in. He'd refused to tell me when the interview was to take place, but I'd found it in the secretaries' notes. I had brought champagne with me— which was probably a bit of a jinx considering what happened the last time we drank together—planning on celebrating with him when he got out. When we'd both be Fellows. Some premonition had told me to keep back and watch him before I approached, in case something went wrong.

I had been right.

There wasn't much I could have done to comfort him. Especially since *I* had succeeded where he had yet to. Since that night two weeks earlier, things had been strained between us. I wish I could remember what happened, curse the tempting green fairy! I should have known better than to pull out the absinthe when he visited me at the lab late that night. I should have stopped when the world started turning even if the liquid was the same colour as his eyes. I couldn't help but drink it in. When I awoke, tucked into the cot, with a headache that throbbed with every beat of my heart and my stomach in knots, he wasn't anywhere to be found.

When he turned away my visits the day after his rejection, I assumed he was simply hard at work to prove them wrong and thus too busy to see me—it had happened before. After a week it was clear that something else was the matter. Something I'd done had driven him away even if he refused to tell me what it was, refused to let me make amends.

So I watched him walk away from the failed interview without comforting him. My presence would have only made things worse.

And when Peter called on me the next day to tell me the news, that "strange little Wilford" wouldn't be joining us in the esteemed halls of the Society, I pictured crushing his nose. Luckily, this time he didn't linger for hours rambling; he had too many people to tell.

The next day I received news that Wilford had left onboard a Navy ship. It's kept me up most of the night. I really thought I had done the right thing in waiting for him to come to me, waiting for him to try again. Giving him space.

I thought we had time.

I guess he can still surprise me.

Maybe this is a good thing, a chance to clear his head, a kind of grand tour. He can come back and reapply in a year or two. Although the rumours of pirates on the coast do worry me.

I keep telling myself there's nothing I could have done differently to convince him to stay. I hope that is true.

June 25th, 1760

LETTER FROM WILFORD BOWEN TO JEAN BAPTISTE DE BEAUPRÉ

JEAN-BAPTISTE,

My sincerest apologies for the delay between letters. Before I begin, I want to assure you that I am *fine*—in fact, you could say I am in quite good spirits considering recent events!

I'm afraid I found myself in quite the predicament—but it's been sorted out now. My ship was boarded by a group of what I soon learned were pirates, on the hunt for a new physician and supplies. They ignored my protestations (that I am not a general physician nor a surgeon even if I can read Latin) and simply carted me onboard with the guns and food as if I were no more than a piece of equipment.

The pirates cut quite a different mien from the Navy officers. Gone are the uniforms and clean cut hair—facial hair, wild locks, and mismatched apparel abound. And I must say the odour of my new shipmates packs quite the punch, especially since they seem more open to spend time in my presence!

I try not to think too much about the men I left behind on the

Navy ship. I could still see it after sunset, burning on the horizon. Good thing we were always first-rate at Latin, Jean.

As it happens, their cook/doctor—a man named Quinton—was sick. I could hear him screaming as soon as I stepped foot on the vessel. They had taken him from his kitchen cot and put him in the second mate's room because it had a door, but the thin wooden walls weren't making much of a difference. His anguished cries were keeping the crew up, although they were no worse than I'd heard in operating theatres at school.

He was lying down when I entered. I could see black pulsing dots all over his arms and legs. I wasn't sure if what I was seeing was a byproduct of sea sickness (being at sea is nothing like rowing in the canal, let me tell you), or a hallucination. But as I got closer, I saw the black spots were holes. They were too small and the light too dim, so I couldn't quite make out what was inside, even crouched above them.

Luckily, Quinton had a beautiful bleeding kit by his side. I used it to slice across a couple of holes, widening their aperture. The blood that leaked out was normal in colour and viscosity. I enticed the lantern-wielding cabin boy to assist me, giving him some sweets stolen from the Navy ship before my—kidnapping? Conscription? Whatever you wish to call it.

With the wounds brightly lit, I saw a flash of white amongst the red. A larvae?

When I tried to pull it out, it squirmed deeper and disappeared. Moments later, a darker juvenile walked past the same hole. A raised bump on Quentin's flesh showing its path as it moved subcutaneously.

I needed to extract samples to get a closer look. I cut again, deeper this time, pulling apart the flesh with my hands. I unveiled a black insect, likely the adult form of the larvae and juvenile I'd seen earlier. Its two antennae sprang forth, red eyes focusing on me. Its black body squirmed out of the hole I had made, using its legs to pull itself out, wings unfurling. It shook off the blood like a wet dog before taking flight.

The insect wasn't much bigger than my thumbnail and was covered in black and red stripes. Wasplike, two stingers of the same length emerged from its pea-sized abdomen. A stunning creature! And one yet to be described by science — I had never heard of parasitic insect adults emerging fully formed from the place their eggs hatched! I wondered if it was seeking a new host in which to lay its eggs.

Quite different from the moths you study, right chap? Ha!

I was lost in admiration until someone tugged me back and thrust a torch where I had been mere moments ago, setting the doctor/cook aflame. I'd heard that the sea was a wild place, but to burn a man alive felt like a cruelty that didn't belong in this world. His screams grew even louder, accompanied by crackling and snapping (Fat? Hair? The insects?) At first, the sulphurous smell of burning hair and acrid odour of flaming clothes filled the cabin, then came a meaty whiff of cooking human flesh. Insects were emerging from his skin, burning up as they met the flames. I felt one crawling on my leg. A crewman splattered the specimen before I had a chance to collect it.

The crew set about swiftly clobbering the insects, some with bare hands, others with shoes or shirts. It was over relatively quickly, and the chef/doctor's charred body was thrown overboard in case anything had survived the flames. A hook-handed man led a rendition of the former cook's favourite ditty, a rather bawdy tale about drinking he'd taught the crew after joining. There was a scandalous rhyme with "Cup" I'm unlikely to forget, but I won't copy it here and sully your eyes.

I was keen to try to save some samples of the charred insect corpses for study, but the Captain made us throw them out with the cook. He said he'd seen some assumed-dead wasps' nests start buzzing after several quiet years and valued the life of his crew more than my "scientific tomfoolery." Even if I could not gather enough evidence about this parasitic wasp to write a paper, I know that with enough time, I should be able to find more wonderful creatures. Maybe I will even write a book about my travels! Just like Robinson Crusoe! But with more wildlife.

I feel that this is the right path. Just as I felt that I had to travel the sea.

I've been given the job of cook/doctor. I'm not much of either but I accepted. A couple crewmates snickered, saying it was "not a choice," but I saw that as light-humoured ribbing. It's not like I'd be sent to walk the plank if I said no. I tried to get the first mate, a man named Huxley, to draw me the fruit they had seen the bugs nesting in, but he just drew a circle and shrugged. I will try to find another person on the crew to make illustrations of my findings. Whoever made the snake tattoos on Barlowe, the master gunner who squashed the specimen that had been crawling on me, has artistic talent. I wonder if he's onboard.

I cut out a couple of eggs from some of the crew's flesh which the Captain confiscated. Some were thankful for my intervention, others cursed in ways I never even thought possible. I'd share them but they'd make even you blush.

Yours,
WB

P.S. I figure, since you'll never be on a pirate ship, I'll describe it to you. Paint you a word picture, if you will.

Turns out it's quite similar to a Navy ship. I mean, there are only so many ways you can make a ship. It's the same mast, the same living quarters and mess.

At the prow, there's a rather impressive figurehead, but instead of a buxom mermaid carved by a master woodworker, it's a rather flat-chested creature with a tail that splits numerous spiralling tendrils. It's distinctive. Meant to evoke octopi, perhaps? However, its mantle resembles that of a jellyfish. When I asked the cabin boy Tommy about it, he said it was the "Sea Goddess," which is also the name of the ship.

For the most part, I can roam freely—although I've yet to be allowed into what the Captain calls the "treasure room," which I'm not to enter "under any circumstance, no matter what you hear."

Every once in a while I see men coming out looking dazed but happy. I'm starting to think they store opium and rum there.

June 30th, 1760

LETTER FROM WILFORD BOWEN TO JEAN BAPTISTE DE BEAUPRÉ

BETWEEN THE RAIDS, battles and everyday illnesses of the crew, I've been quite busy. Sorry for the lack of letters (although we've yet to land at a port where I can send them to you). I've been working hard, worried that the Captain might toss me to the depths for incompetence. Compared to Quinton (may he rest in watery peace) who was a better chef than a doctor (but only marginally), I can read medicine labels, set bones, and treat wounds. Not a night goes by without some crew member showing me a strange wound or rumbling stomach and begging for a remedy! I am rarely lonely or bored, which is quite a contrast to the Navy ship.

Is there a paper published on common illnesses of pirates? I would assume not, as there isn't much scholarly interest in such a thing. In any case, here are my findings:

Captain Samson: Refused examination but seems hale other than a persistent cough. Smokes like a chimney.

1st Mate and Quartermaster, Huxley: Slightly bow-legged from childhood illness.

Second Mate, Edric: The usual collection of scars from battle, three missing fingers, and a missing toe. A split toenail grew twistingly in two opposite directions like the horns of a goat. It was so thick I had to use Wyatt's woodworking tools to trim it.

Boatswain, Wyatt: A rather concerning mole growth the size of a fist out of his side. He refuses to let me cut off, calling it "his wife Deborah."

Cabin Boy, Tommy Tomkin: Undernourished, neither of us is sure of his age. Rather speedy and agile, with an uncanny ability to vanish whenever the doctoring tasks are especially rank or goopy.

Master Gunner, Barlowe: Relatively hale and very strong. I feel like he could easily throw me overboard if he set his mind to it, but he doesn't strike me as a man to lose his temper with the crew.

Assorted other crew/deck hands:

Darby: A rather advanced case of syphilis, treated with daily applications of mercury. His nose has started to show signs of blackening and will soon fall off. I regret not having access to the prosthetic noses we have in England, but he seems unbothered, assuring me it will make him look more fearsome in battle.

Joshua: The crew's resident osprey, always standing high up on the sails. Surprisingly little evidence of broken bones, although he has a rather impressive rope burn scar on his arm. And a nasty case of syphilis.

Lindsay: Missing half his teeth, the rest are cracked. A thumb-sized splinter in his left thigh. Several badly set broken fingers. Loss of hearing in his right ear. I would not be shocked if someone told me they stuff this man into a cannon and launch him at enemy vessels.

Mac: Left hand lost in battle and replaced by a hook. I thought this was just a legend! He swears his was made by melting down the sword from the one who gave him the injury. When asked what became of the rest of the man, he patted his stomach and winked at me. He might be lying, but I have no real proof either way.

Christopher: The tallest of the crew by a good few inches. Walks with a slight limp and complains of back pain, likely because he has to bend in half anytime he is below decks.

While each member of the crew seems to have their own unique combination of illnesses and ailments, all those I've treated bear weird circular bruises. Whenever I ask to look at these wounds more closely, they push me away and tell me not to worry—which is strange since they love to show off all their other ailments, battle scars especially, which are displayed as proudly as art in a stately home.

Perhaps it is a sign of another parasitic infestation or a case of ringworm. Or they might be caused by cupping—although I did not find any of the necessary implements in the medical kit, and no other crew possesses the medical knowledge required for such a procedure. I will keep trying to get a closer look when they're shirtless.

The things I do for science!

Yours,
Wilford

July 3rd, 1760

LETTER FROM WILFORD BOWEN TO JEAN BAPTISTE DE BEAUPRÉ

CAPTAIN SAMSON THINKS it's unseemly for me to cower during raids and says he should not have to worry about a defenceless, lily-livered landlubber if we get boarded. So Barlowe has been tasked with teaching me the basics of swashbuckling.

That's been taking up my mornings, and when I'm done preparing food, I'm subjected to callisthenics and then repeatedly told to "thrust" while holding a sword. I can imagine you holding in a laugh but smiling in that quiet way you have.

Master Gunner Barlowe does cut (ha ha!) an impressive figure. I've gotten a much better look at those snake tattoos I had glimpsed when he was waving his shirt around to kill the flying parasitic wasps. He'd been moving around so much then that it had been hard to get a good look. But now, as he demonstrates proper technique ("block and thrust, thrust!") I see them much more clearly. He has several snakes that wind themselves around his arms and torso and continue below his waistband. They are extraordinarily detailed—down to the outline of the scales—compared to the blurry and faded tattoos on the rest of the crew. Their eyes are a startling purple pigment that seems to almost glow against his tanned skin.

He's also very strong, I believe the boys at school called it "barrel-chested." I doubt I could wrap my arms around him if I tried.

Not that I would, of course.

Anyway, he found me a machete and after many manual adjustments of my posture, he said I might be ready for a cutlass soon enough. He promised to keep an eye out during raids for something that "might suit."

I'm terribly sore from the whole venture. I feel muscles I'd seen in anatomical texts or on more muscular types like Barlowe but had no evidence I'd possessed until now. My trapezius is particularly tender, and there's a muscle in my armpit that tingles every time I reach for supplies on a shelf. I'm quite sure it has yet to be discovered by science and seems to have no purpose but to torture me. Unfortunately, Tommy never seems to be around when I need to lift supply crates (although I could swear I hear his chuckles as I grunt and groan).

Barlowe assures me the pain will fade, has offered to massage the ache out of my tired arms if it becomes too much. At least he doesn't laugh at me when I struggle with a sword like the rest of the crew does.

He promised that I'm almost ready for the practice dummy and showed me a burlap and straw mannequin, with a rather convincingly painted grimace.

Barlowe gave the dummy a punch and it squeaked. He assured me it was "just because of mice," but even my sceptical mind can't help but wonder if being transformed into a dummy isn't the fate of a disobedient crewman.

Being on the seas for this short while is clearly turning me into a superstitious person, just like the rest of the crew. Joshua always bends over to tickle his toes before leaping onto the masts; he says it gives him a better grip. Huxley prays every morning, but curiously when I commented about my surprise at there being Protestant pirates, he said "that isn't my God." Barlowe kisses his cannons for good luck. Crewmates ask him whether it's cheating now that he has a new beau, although I'm not sure who they are referring to.

On the topic of changes, I've developed a suntan. Well, it was a rather bad peeling burn, but it's settling into a golden brown. I doubt you'd recognize me if you saw me, especially dressed in my pirate garb.

I wonder what you'd think of me...

~~I hope you would be impressed by these recent developments and not disappointed by my inability to join the Royal Society.~~

It really hasn't all been bad days or hard work. In fact, just last night, Barlowe showed me something quite incredible.

When he woke me up with a hand over my mouth, I was worried that we had gotten boarded. I'd been dreaming of an army of practice dummies squeaking as they surrounded me. But instead, Barlowe gleefully beckoned me onto the moonlit deck.

At first, I wanted to ask why he had bothered to wake me. But then I noticed how the light was quite a bit greener than usual and, despite the moon being a sliver in the sky, the deck was brightly lit although the shadows were strange, like grasping fingers. It took me a second to realise that the source of the light was different.

Suddenly, as if on cue, a large, luminous fish leapt through the air in front of my eyes!

I ran to the side of the boat, looking down to see huge creatures glowing light green.

Whales! I'd heard tales of these enormous creatures that dwarfed our Navy's largest boats but had never seen one myself!

And I had never heard of them glowing before!

There were maybe a dozen large adults and even more juveniles and babies in the pod. They swam a swirling dance amongst the stars, and the moon reflected on the surface of the water, giving the impression that they were celestial creatures. Their movements were so complex they seemed choreographed. I watched mesmerised until the sun came up and they disappeared into the brightening horizon.

It is hard work being on a pirate ship, even with Tommy the cabin boy's assistance (when he isn't hiding from me). But ... I am happy I left home, and luckier still that I was brought onboard this ship.

I've seen such wonders here even in this short time.

No one on the Navy ship wanted to befriend me; it was a rather lonely, regimented place. But here, even with the brutality, I have made one friend. If only you were here it'd be perfect. I'm curious what kind of figure you'd cut in these pirate garbs, waving a sword around...

Yours,
Wilford

July 5th, 1760

ENTRY FROM JEAN BAPTISTE DE BEAUPRÉ'S JOURNAL

THE SOCIETY WAS in a great upheaval when I arrived at the General Meeting. I thought at first that someone had uncovered another scandal (perhaps another stolen notebook or more fabricated findings), but no.

I am not sure how to feel.

Willie is alive. But the worst has come to pass: He was kidnapped by pirates.

Only he could manage to get himself into this much trouble.

At least he isn't dead—it's a bit of hope—but I wonder how he'll survive. He's not accustomed to hardship or the cruelties of life. He could barely take care of himself in England, often too caught up in studying to bathe. I'd often joked that if it weren't for me, he'd have never reached his twenties, but now because of me he's left Britain only to fall in with criminals and killers.

Will I ever learn what I did wrong and make amends?

What will come of him being in among a crew of such ill-repute? And how will he ever join law-abiding society again? The piracy charges will cling to him for the rest of his (likely short) life.

I only hope he tries to come back home as soon as he can.

Will I hear from him again?

His presence in my world was a constant, and now that he's gone, I find myself lost in memories, the only place he still resides.

I keep revisiting the memory of our first meeting.

For several weeks I had been gathering rowan leaves from around the Oxford campus to feed to my moths. Just a few here and there, nothing too extreme or which could damage the trees. I collected them from quiet parts of the gardens, away from the bustle of students, where I could clear my head.

When collecting one morning, I felt the neck tingling pin-pricks of someone quietly observing me. Before I could turn to greet this stranger, his lilting voice spoke.

"If I may, the stems are easier to cut from an angle." His hands came around to mine, guiding my shears to snip a stem before pulling away. "See? Much cleaner this way. I've been collecting the same samples for my snails, they're hungry little ones, so I've had to develop some harvesting techniques. You know, I've never seen you harvesting around here before. I'm Wilford."

I turned to find a short man, sandy haired with a crooked smile and a twinkle in his eye. He spoke so quickly and covered such a range of topics it left my head spinning. He told me of his snails, and I shared my moths in return. He asked if he could see them.

And just like that—he became a steadfast friend. I can scarcely believe we haven't known each other since birth. We took our meals together daily near the big window that framed the Tom Tower, discussing lectures and our research. After only a month, he could predict my line of thinking before it left my mouth—making our conversations extremely hard to follow for anyone else within earshot. He would often rush up to me after Zoology lectures, a scribbled note clutched in his hand, an idea so pressing it couldn't wait for hellos. I'd tell him to slow down, his words falling from his mouth out of order, as if tumbling over each other.

It's one of the things I miss the most.

My studies of moths just don't hold my attention anymore—I've hit a dead end. When the pupae are left to naturally hatch from their cocoons, they release a chemical that breaks down the layers so they can wiggle free. This leaves a residue that is difficult to separate from the raw silk and lowers the quality of the thread (which is much more important to the merchants than the slaughter of humble moths). I just know my Wil would find a solution for this. As frustrated as I am, I know that my pursuit of them is necessary for my continued admittance into the Royal Society. But without Willie and his earnest enthusiasm at my side, my interest is fading. He has been a guiding force in my own scientific enquiry. Discussing theories with him well into the night, sharing our findings...

I know he would want me to continue. So I will. Even if my heart aches.

July 6th, 1760

LETTER FROM WILFORD BOWEN TO JEAN BAPTISTE DE BEAUPRÉ

DEAREST JEAN,

Do you want the good news or the bad news first?

That's a silly question to ask in a letter but it is just as silly to ask you in person, even if I did it often. I was always charmed by your deep-honeyed voice saying "whatever is more interesting" as if you wouldn't listen keenly to every boring story I told.

I'll start at the beginning.

We raided a Navy ship.

Well, "we" excludes the one writing. The Captain still isn't entirely convinced that I won't stick myself with the pointy end of a sword, despite Barlowe's careful lessons. He's also not in the mood to find another doctor/chef, although I'm not much of the latter, as you'll see shortly.

We lost Christopher the giant in the raid, dead before he made it back to the *Goddess*. But we also got some new crew from the ship, so we ended up with more than we started with. Scottie seems nice, another boatswain to help Wyatt with his tasks. The two are already fast friends (just like we were!) There are also the twins, Hobbs and Barnaby, who even have matching mirror-image scars from their temples to their cheeks. It's really the only way to tell them apart.

There's also Henry, an older fellow who keeps to himself.

In addition to the crew, we got their cache of food, which was great since we were starting to run low on supplies. They had some fresh fruit and a barrel of crustaceans caught on a nearby island. The queue at dinner that first night was particularly boisterous, as the men hadn't eaten fresh meat in a week at least—Lindsay lost a tooth biting into a particularly smelly, stiff dried sausage—and had been complaining loudly the last couple of days. Mac had—jokingly?— threatened to cut my legs off and eat me like ham if I didn't deliver "the goods" soon.

Crisis averted, thanks to the lobster bucket.

While my first few attempts to cook the lobsters turned out quite tough, by the end of the line, I managed one that pleased even the picky Captain. I'd heard that lobster was quite repulsive—they were fed to inmates at the old Bailey after all—but the crew were so excited that I ended up sampling some myself and thought it was a little chewy but quite delicious. And it was fresh!

Or so we thought.

I know I promised you some bad news. Well, it's coming.

The next day, when I opened the lid, the lobsters looked lethargic, like the crew when they were falling over each other after a night of excessive alcohol consumption. At first, I was happy about this development, having had to treat Tommy's broken finger yesterday after he'd failed to wrangle a feisty lobster. My best assistant could not stand to lose a digit in a kitchen casualty.

I could hear grumblings from the mess as the crew started to eat, but that wasn't unusual. I just hoped the Captain wouldn't deliver on his threat to turn me into shark feed so "I might give someone else indigestion for a change."

When I grabbed the next lobster from the bucket, I could tell something was wrong: its abdomen was hollowed out, the grey carapace half gone and what was left of its mass of colourful entrails dribbled out where the tail should be. I wrote it off as a simple case of cannibalism—there wasn't anything else to eat in there but each other. I took a mental note, in case the behaviour had yet to be observed. I placed the presumed-dead lobster on my table for future study and resumed my cooking duties.

Several specimens later, I found another one with a similarly hollow carapace, its tail holding on by the smallest sliver of keratin.

Unlike the stillness of the other lobster, this one waved its claws at me (albeit weakly). At first, I thought I had caught it in its final moments, the second wind of a dying man. I turned to place this dying lobster with his compatriot.

But the table was empty.

I felt a tug at my pant leg and looked down to see the first lobster, ribbons of entrails trailing behind it. I nudged it away with my foot but it walked back towards me with the mien of a drunk man trying to convince you he's sober. It tried to pinch me again but I pushed it back with the long spoon ladle.

"Uh, Doc?" I turned to the door to see one of the new crew, Mark, turning as green as I had been my first week at sea. I dodged the vomit that arced towards me.

The lobster was not as agile. It didn't seem to mind though, even as puke filled its carapace.

"I feel sick," the man stated rather obviously before passing out.

I had a hunch and ran into the mess shouting at everyone to stop eating immediately. Some of the new men sneered at me, ignoring my advice, biting into the white flesh of the crustaceans I'd cooked up.

The foolish tend to die young, I suspect this might have something to do with it.

The Captain looked down at the cooked lobster in his hands. It twitched weakly despite having been boiled. The ship's rocking often sent our food tumbling across our plates, but the waves below us did not drive this movement—the food itself was animated. He spat out his meal before following me back into the kitchen.

"You said the Captain and Second Mate of the other ship were both lethargic, right?" I asked.

"You think these lobsters had something to do with it?"

I grabbed the floor lobster, tipping out the contents of its cara-

THE FLESH OF THE SEA

pace easily avoiding its weakly snapping claws, and placed it on the table. We both leaned in to get a closer look (the Captain with his usual grim determination and me with, as you should know, giddy enthusiasm and a barely contained squeal). This was a new discovery! I was sure of it! How was this lobster still moving? What mechanisms could keep a creature alive despite its guts being exposed to the open air, or being cooked as the Captain's had been? Such a thing would be of immense interest to the Royal Society! There'd be no denying my entrance then.

As I got in close, I saw a strand, which was not much wider than a hair, grow out of the abdominal cavity, sprouting five or so centimetres (I really should keep a ruler on me at all times) over the course of about a minute. A little bulb grew at its tip, which I later realised was a slime mould's sprouting body.

The bulb pulsed once, like the pounding of a heart.

The Captain pulled me away before a grey cloud emerged from the tip. The miniscule spores spread over several feet in all directions, reaching where my face had been before the Captain's intervention. The smell of spoiled fish filled the kitchen and we both brought our shirts over our noses instinctually.

I noticed then that the lobster had stopped moving.

As had Mark.

We watched him for a moment, unsure if he would share the lobster's fate or whether he had died — too complex for reanimation.

With a hard jerk, he got to his feet, steadying himself with a hand that sizzled as it landed on the cauldron's edge. He did not flinch or react in any way to something that must have been incredibly painful. I could smell his flesh cooking (not altogether different from the smell of pork or the odour that had come from Quinton).

This creature made the recipient impervious to pain and allowed them to continue moving even after death! Forget the Royal Society, I'd be knighted for this, I was sure!

How would you like to call me "Sir"?

I mean...

All I mean is that even my parents would be impressed.

The Captain, however, was not.

He pulled his sabre and sliced the crewman's head right off, a geyser of blood painting my kitchen crimson. The body collapsed through the open door. Those in the mess screamed as the headless corpse twitched and tried standing up. It slipped in its blood and fell back down.

It was absolutely remarkable! The possibilities were endless!

The Captain was cursing as the corpse tried to move again. Clearly, he had thought his swift blow would be enough to fell the creature.

Barlowe stumbled into view and saw the chaos: the twitching man, the Captain with his sabre out, and me. No telling what I looked like at this point. Probably quite fearsome coated in blood as I was.

"Help me toss it overboard, quickly!" the Captain said as he grabbed the head and Barlowe snatched the gently wiggling corpse. Already, thin golden hair-like strands were growing where a head used to stand. The process seemed to be affecting the crew member much faster than it had the crustaceans, and I shouted at the two men to let me have a closer look. Especially since these bulbous sporocysts seemed much larger and more defined than the ones that came out of the lobster.

I was ignored.

Barlowe and the Captain threw the corpse pieces into the sea just as the strands burst.

It sank into the waves and I could do nothing but watch as yet another marvellous specimen, yet another key to the glorious halls in which you sit, was lost to science. Moments later, the Captain reappeared at my side, tossing the lobster bucket into a watery grave.

Even after my great scientific loss, I had to clean the kitchen and come up with another meal. And the crew were starving and grumpy since I gave all those who had eaten the tainted meat purgatives, even if no one else was showing symptoms. I assured them vomiting and hunger was worse than death.

Clearly, my issue will not be finding specimens of scientific value, but rather keeping my Captain from destroying everything we find.

He seems to be as great an enemy of scientific progress as he is of the Royal Navy.

Later, going through Mark's personal effects, I found something curious. The insignia on his uniform marked him as the second mate. He had likely disguised himself as a member of the crew, knowing pirates usually dispatched high-ranking individuals when capturing ships. That explained why the new crew had been so deferent to him and let him have the larger meals. He might have been eating lobster for days before we had picked him up inadvertently. Thus, the process hadn't been faster; he had just been eating the lobsters longer than the others.

But that will forever remain an untested theory since my evidence has sunk to the bottom of the sea.

Oh, I promised you good news!

Barlowe found me a cutlass! He's promised me more lessons now that I have a weapon of my own. To be honest, I'm not sure if the blade is of high quality, but he sharpened it to the point where I jokingly used it to chop some potatoes before he confiscated it—he was concerned for my "useful little fingers."

Hope you are keeping well!
WB

P.S. The Captain decided to stop off at Lisbon to trade spices and dyes for food after the whole "lobster debacle." Barlowe offered to get my letters onboard a ship on its way back to England. I'm not sure if you'll get these and when, but I imagine you reading them with your eyebrows ever so slightly raised, probably thinking I'm pulling your tail. Hope all is well in Mother England!

July 20th, 1760

ENTRY FROM JEAN BAPTISTE DE BEAUPRÉ'S JOURNAL

WHEN THE POSTMAN arrived with a large stack of paper tied with twine and demanded a rather ludicrous fee, I thought the boys at the Society were pranking me again. (They'd been quite vicious lately, wearing pirate hats and asking me if I was so glum because Wilford had "shivered my timbers.") But then I saw the handwriting: Wilford's looping chicken scratch.

He's alive! Well, he was still alive as of July 6th—so, two weeks ago.

While a part of me is delighted that he seems to be doing well (all things considered) and has forgiven me enough to send updates, I'm also worried that he does not seem to want to return, instead obstinately pursuing his foolish quest to prove himself to the Society. I worry he will not flee from danger but instead willingly run towards it, hoping to learn more, gather proof to impress those stuffy old men. The glee with which he paints such terrifying encounters is characteristic—I can't help but miss him for it. But this endearing trait is also the greatest danger.

The creatures he describes seem impossible. I know tales of

animals from faraway lands, like elephants and tigers, seemed just as unlikely but were eventually proven to be real when specimens made their way to our hallowed halls. But these seem so much stranger, even more unlikely than a beast larger than a carriage with giant ears and a hose-like nose. Some of Wilford's discoveries would shock the scientific community for decades to come—if they didn't immediately denounce Willie as a hoaxer and a madman, which I fear would likely be the case.

If he wasn't first hung for piracy.

I'm also unsure how to respond, or even if I can. I've no address, no future destinations. He's the one at sea and yet it is I who feels lost in the ocean's expanse, the unfathomable distance between us growing each day. And there is nothing I can do to get him back.

Of course I believe he *is* actually encountering these animals; my Wil has never been a good liar. I worry for his safety. It's in his nature to hold the scientific value of his samples above his own well-being. If he survives—I hope he survives—and with a lot of luck, the specimens might have enough scientific value to impress the Royal Society and justify his pirating.

Perhaps that's wishful thinking.

I wish I could have studied birds so I could tie a message to one's leg, pleading Wilford to come home. My moths are much too fragile to undergo such a perilous journey.

My research into these tiny, delicate creatures and how to create my own silk while leaving the moths alive is a childish endeavour to most. The lives of these insects don't matter in the end. I'm in favour with the Society only for the benefits I offer when inspecting goods from The Orient—thus, for lining their pockets. Only Wilford truly cared for creatures as I do.

I miss him so.

July 20th, 1760

LETTER FROM WILFORD BOWEN TO JEAN BAPTISTE DE BEAUPRÉ

DEAREST JEAN,

I did not intend the tardiness in dispatching this letter to you. I promise everything is alright, there was just a bit of a mishap. All sorted now. A most extraordinary discovery! However, in the process, we were unable to retrieve any kind of specimen for reasons I will get into.

We made a scheduled stop at a small island inhabited by Indigenous peoples of the region. The Captain regularly trades with them, and it gives the crew a chance to stretch their legs. I admit I was quite relieved to touch the good Earth again, to distance myself from the smells of the sea, if only briefly. My "sea legs" hold no comparison to those like Barlowe, Joshua, and Lindsay who have been sailing their whole lives.

Around midday, I explored the jungle outskirts, armed with a machete—don't worry, my friend, I was well-prepared! I discovered a path, worn from years of use. It twisted through the trees and was clearly maintained because there were no protruding branches or ferns. I followed it to an open clearing where a series of altars surrounded a perfectly round cave entrance at least twice my height in diameter. Leftover food and animal skins were set out for what looked like ritual purposes, next to small statues of a creature resembling a centipede spiralling upwards with massive pincers or tusks. I stepped into the cavern entrance itself, noting concave ridges spanning the circumference every few feet. The pathway descended into the earth with a slight decline. Joshua saw me entering the cave and pulled me out by the scruff of my shirt, telling me there was danger within. He lugged me back to the village despite my protestations and kept mum about what lived in the depths.

Trade was well underway when we reached the crew and Indigenous folks who were engaging in some lighthearted bartering. The villagers spoke a mixture of languages, perhaps to facilitate trade. I could decipher a bit of French (I admit I thought of you, hearing it, my dear), Portuguese, Spanish, and what I believe to be their native tongue. It was fascinating to hear them switch between each, sometimes in the middle of sentences! Spirits were high and, after business concluded, we shared an evening meal of hunted boar, roasted fruits, and bottled rum from the ship.

Following our meal, the chieftain joined us as we gathered close around the fire. I turned to young Tommy and asked him if he knew about the cave. Unexpectedly, the chief pointed his cane at me and responded in English! "Important Place," he told us. A few other locals nodded in agreement. A call went up to tell of the "Great Worm." Mac elbowed me in the stomach and explained this was a local legend, one retold during every visit. While I'm not sure I received an exact translation, here is what the crew told me:

A sea worm, known as The Drudge—became bored with the endless waves. He rose up, shaking His carapace to create islands. The Great Worm then wandered the lands for millennia, creating animals and man. Content with His life, and weary, He chose to burrow underground and sleep for eternity. It is said if the Worm awakens again, the Earth will shake and rumble.

A few of the younger villagers, strapping young lads on the cusp of adulthood, bragged about having gone inside the cave as a test of courage, each goading the others to tread deeper and deeper. Marks on their arms showed how far they had gone, one ring for every indentation in the cave walls they passed. Those having travelled to the greatest depths and bearing the most rings were paid the highest respect. The chief lifted his arm, displaying at least double the marks of anyone in the village, more than I could count in the short flash we were granted.

It is even required to prove one's worth before one can marry. Wyatt laughed along with the villagers and puffed out his chest at the other men, especially Scottie. These two were always trying to outdo each other. The local women were as polite as the ladies in Britain when dealing with such buffoonery. I had to smile. Some things are the same no matter where you are in the world.

For the rest of the night, the crew spoke of the caves and little else. The twins, Hobbs and Barnaby, always competitive, each vowed to go deeper than the other. Lindsay and Darby egged them on, promising to be witnesses to the contest. Joshua said they were all daredevils, and when the crew pointed out how he spent his days on dangerously swaying masts above the water, he said, "yes but that's up *above* ground and not inside it," as if that was explanation enough for his reluctance. Barlowe, deep in his cups, asked me how far I wanted him to go—his drunken cheeks flushed red. He ignored me when I asked for clarification. Mac then repeated his statement and the two play-fought in the bush for, as Mac put it, "my honour." The Captain, Huxley and Edric talked some sense into a party of our men who intended to head into the cave, convincing them instead to sleep off their drink. It would do them no good to stumble into the darkness drunk when we had to leave in the morning.

It was warm enough that most men slept outside under the stars. I looked up at them and realised that these are the same stars you see, Jean. Do you think of me when you gaze towards the sky?

I awoke the next morning to several people yelling. Wyatt, as you might have already guessed, had absconded to the cave during the early hours. Scottie professed he thought the other man was joking when he said he'd "wanted to prove himself," but when he woke,

Wyatt was nowhere to be found. He was likely still drunk when the idea occurred.

The local men who had been inside the cave before offered to accompany us and lead the way. They armed themselves with spears while the crew grabbed pistols and clubs. The Captain was furious but refused to leave a man behind. (They have become increasingly hard to keep lately, with our string of unfortunate encounters.) Still filled with liquid courage from the night before, I was carried along by the wave, head spinning as we trod through the humid underbrush for several kilometres. I lost track of our expedition for a moment when I stopped to admire a brilliant pheasant with feathers surpassing even the peafowl specimens of the Royal Society—only to be tugged along by Darby who had come back to find me.

When we reached the tunnel, the crew separated into groups. The Captain, Scottie, Darby, Hobbs, Barnaby and myself plus a half dozen villagers entered the cave while Huxley and Tommy, Mac and the others stood watch outside. Then the Captain loudly declared any crew member seen removing items from the altar would be shot on sight. I admire his respect for these tribesmen; he is a good man.

Hobbs was not much more than three feet into the tunnel when he called out, "Wyatt!"

A villager covered Hobbs' mouth, whispering harshly. The Captain translated for us even if the message was clear. "He says shut your mouth. Sound down here will wake the Drudge."

We did as ordered, solemnly walked three men abreast into the darkness. Torches illuminated only our close vicinity—beyond was pitch blackness. The uniformity of the rock formation felt unnatural, made in a way that set my skin on edge. As we travelled deeper, I could have sworn the walls were closing in on us, despite taking measurements which provided proof of the contrary. I have never journeyed into the Earth before and believe it contrary to my constitution. I did not belong there. None of us did.

Some ways into our descent, perhaps a mile, the paths diverged, and so likewise we split into smaller groups. Darby left a coat where the cave split to help guide us back and to cool himself. He was sweating profusely and complained of the heat, and I admit I was beginning to feel as if we were entering Hell itself.

A scream from Scottie echoed down the shaft. He clutched Wyatt's bandanna, torn and sullied. Several crew members including the Captain placed a hand on his shoulder to console the poor lad.

Our grief was quickly interrupted by a deep rumbling, what I can only describe as the Earth moaning. The trembling reverberated in my ears as if they were connected to the stone walls. Those around me yelled and shoved in a panic as they fled. I was knocked around, and by the time I regained my feet, I was no longer sure which way led to the exit and took off in a random direction. I tripped on one of the rings, dropping my torch so I could catch myself on the wall. The rumbling got louder, dirt and rocks raining down on me from above. I was about to cower and protect my head when I heard my name being called from a small crevice to the side of the tunnel.

Wyatt!

He reached out for me, I thought for an embrace, but instead he tugged me to him, his eyes wide as saucers while pulling me into his hiding spot. I asked how he survived, but he put his finger to his lips.

We were not alone.

A rich, loamy smell entered my nostrils. The rumbling continued for a moment, then stopped, replaced by a wet, masticating gurgle. I could not help myself—I craned my head out from our hiding place.

I beheld the worm. It had a hard exterior of overlapping scales. Its muscular system and waves of scales must have allowed it to travel at great speeds; it had sprung upon us at a remarkable pace. This creature had clearly dug the tunnel—its body fit perfectly inside the wall, like fingers in a tailored glove. Perhaps the folklore was based in fact.

The Drudge slithered snugly through the depths and lay just past where I stood moments before. Slightly translucent, the organs were visible, its glassy carapace displaying a series of hearts that pumped synchronously inside its abdomen. It raised its head, its eyes no bigger than pinheads, likely an adaptation to darkness. Two long feelers retracted into the mouthparts. A host of antennae carefully palpitated the walls and floor. Smelling the remnants of our sweat, perhaps? The carapace was a deep purple, iridescent in the light of my fallen torch.

It gradually moved closer and closer to our hiding spot. Wyatt was holding on to me so tightly I had bruises later. Suddenly, the Drudge smashed full force into the wall just to our left!

It had picked up our scent!

The worm pressed itself against the crevice, thrashing violently and attempting to grab us with its feelers. We were both screaming and looking around for something to attack it with. Wyatt pointed to the torch, or at the gap between it and the worm. It had twisted its body to avoid the flames! I grabbed at the light, fumbling before gripping it with both hands and thrusting it into the soft tissues surrounding the mouth. It spasmed and recoiled immediately, retreating back into the depths from which it came.

We waited until we no longer felt the rumblings. Then Wyatt insisted we remain a bit longer, just to be sure. He was hysterical at this point. I had to tug him out of our hiding spot. He cowered at every noise until we emerged into the harsh sunlight. The crew greeted us, Barlowe gathering me up in a bone-crushing hug while Mac—holding my doctoring bag—made a point to count all of our limbs and declared us hale. I explained what we saw, although they were less excited by my descriptions of the Drudge than I had hoped. Scottie ran to Wyatt and embraced him, the pair sobbing as they reunited. On the walk back, I mourned maiming such a sacred and unique creature. I pray it recovers. I did not tell the Indigenous folk what happened for fear I would be put to death. This secret remains between the two—now three of us, with you included, my friend.

Another feast was held that night, this time honouring Wyatt and myself. The bandanna was hung with other decorative flags over the chief's hut. I remember little of this night; I drank heavily and felt sick for days. As we set off the next sunrise, we were laden with gifts far surpassing the original traded goods—the Captain was pleased.

I hope that you are well.

~~ab imo pectore,~~ Yours,
Wilford

July 25th, 1760

LETTER FROM WILFORD BOWEN TO JEAN BAPTISTE DE BEAUPRÉ

SWEET JEAN,

The most astounding creatures sailed past us today! I must say I was worried at first since our encounters with wildlife have been deadly as of late. However, these were quite peaceful, ethereal even.

"Man O' War spotted ahead!" Joshua cried at midday from his crow's nest.

The excitement from the men was staggering. Were we under attack? No, they were in good spirits. A fellow pirate crew? While unsure, I joined the others. We all peered over the starboard bow, with Hobbs and Barnaby climbing up the sails to see better.

I could not see them well until Huxley offered me a spyglass—I must acquire one of my own someday, Barlowe offered to find me one during our next raid—and it took me a moment to understand what lay on the ocean's surface.

A herd, or pod, of a half dozen—maybe more—enormous jelly-fish bobbed together, carried by the wind. They resembled large sails —hence the name and my initial confusion. Their flotation sacs were just as cerulean as the sky and ocean, a perfect camouflage even with their massive size. A distinctive scarlet stripe along the peak of the "sail" was the only way to discern it among the blues. Joshua has eyes like a hawk.

Mac began tapping his hook on the railing, and soon the crew stomped together in rhythm. I was pleasantly surprised by Mac's timbre, high and sweet and clear.

"There's nought upon the stern,
There's nought upon the lee,"
Blow high, blow low, and so say we;
"But there's a lofty ship to windward
And she's sailing fast and free,"
Cruising down along the coast
Of the High Barbaree.

"O hail her! O hail her!"
Our gallant Captain cried,
Blow high, blow low,
and so say we;
"Are you a man-o-war
Or a privateer?" said he,
Cruising down along the coast
Of the High Barbaree.

"O I am not a man-o-war
Nor privateer," said he;
Blow high, blow low,
and so say we;

"But I'm a salt-sea pirate
Whose a-looking for his fee,"
Cruising down along the coast
Of the High Barbaree.

Look ahead, look a stern,

look the weather in the lee,
Blow high! Blow low!
and so sailed we;
I see a wreck to the windward
and a lofty ship to lee,
A sailing down all on the coasts
Of the High Barbaree.

"O are you a pirate
or a man-o-war?" cried we.
Blow high! Blow low!
and so sailed we;
"O no! I'm not a pirate,
but a man-o-war," cried he.
A sailing down all on the coasts
Of the High Barbaree."

I watched the jellies until they disappeared, blending into the great blue. They say the sea is a harsh mistress, unpredictable, but she is equally beautiful. I wish you could see it, Jean. My letters pale in comparison to nature's glory.

I have to wonder how things are back home. Did my family even notice my departure? They probably relish my leaving; I was always the black sheep. Admittedly—and I'm certain this makes me a terrible son—I do not miss them. Or most of England. The only thing I lack is your company. In my waking thoughts and in my dreams, you are there. How I wish it were real.

All my best,
W

July 29th, 1760

ENTRY FROM JEAN BAPTISTE DE BEAUPRÉ'S JOURNAL

I HAVE COME to realise what a colossal, incompetent fool I've been.

I've never had the courage to be forthright about my feelings for Willie for fear of pushing him away. I settled for the ways things were, as much as it pained me. What was I to do? I couldn't live without him and if I were to make my intentions clear, he might never speak to me again. Instead, I became a stray dog living on scraps, devouring every morsel I could. A smile, a laugh—even just time sitting in his company, each of us with our heads in a book. It was always the two of us and I took great comfort in that, even if we were friends and not lovers. I never shared him with anyone.

Ever since he left, it's like I've lost a limb. Every scientific finding or discovery feels hollow without him to share it with … I'll turn the corner at Oxford and see something (the grizzled old cat munching on a shoe, a lonely page from a book floating in the wind, a pair of lovers cozied on a gondola) that will bring up a long-lost memory and have no one to reminisce with. We had invented our own language through shared memories and experience and, with him gone, I have no one left to speak it to and I'm afraid it will fade with disuse. I have no great adventures to distract me like he does. Instead, I spend my days agonising over his departure and trying to puzzle together what happened that night.

At least I've solved that mystery. It came to me this morning when I found the emptied bottle; the smell on its lip brought back the memory. That night, I had let the drink make me bold. I don't remember exactly what I said... but I remember his lips close, the sugar on the upper bow which I had leaned over to taste. I remember that heart-fluttering moment when he had leaned in before pushing me away. The panicked look on his face... How could I have forgotten?

That face haunts me now. Like the painful afterimage of the sun when you blink.

Maybe I was better off not remembering what happened.

Wil's been gone for just under two months, off to some remote island every other week — God knows where. All I can do is sit thousands of miles away and lament for having pushed him away.

I've read the letters he's sent many, many times each by now. I'm afraid for his life, for his health, but more than that, I'm afraid I'll be replaced in his estimation. Lord above! — he's on a vessel with great beasts of men, tanned of skin and bursting with muscles and energy. How am I to compare to this ... this *Barlowe* gentleman who keeps offering to find him trinkets on raids and "manually adjusting" him during fight training? It's clear that Barlowe shares my dilection, and taste. And Wilford is not pushing this man away; with every letter they seem to be growing closer. I am tortured nightly by dreams of them entwined, coated in each other, sweat, and the sea. My supervisor has started to comment on my sallow skin and jumpiness, and gives me a bitter look as if he knows the cause and disapproves.

Will *mon cher* ever want to return? Gallivanting around with swashbucklers is far more interesting than study hall and research with a silly little Frenchman.

Oh, Wil. We're really in it now, aren't we?

And now, if only we had talked, if only I could have acted

without needing the influence of drink, if only I'd calmly told the man my desire rather than springing it on him unprepared—he might still be here in England. He would still be safe. Oh, Wilford. I am so sorry. My heart weeps.

August 1st, 1760

LETTER FROM WILFORD BOWEN TO JEAN BAPTISTE DE BEAUPRÉ

DEAREST JEAN,

It's been a difficult couple of nights, my hardest so far on the passage.

Staying up all night is much more difficult now than when we were in school. Back then, we had boundless energy to discuss theories and conduct experiments into the small hours of the morning. The rising and setting of the sun just meant we needed more candles. Now, if I sleep badly for one night, I am groggy and irritable the next day. Never mind not sleeping for three!

As the sun was setting, three nights ago, I was cleaning the decks alongside Wyatt and Lindsay when I heard a strange humming. As Lindsay was mostly deaf in his left ear, I asked Wyatt if he heard anything. It took him a minute but then his face blanched and he ran off to find the Captain.

The sound came from dead ahead and resembled a crying child. I looked into the waves below for a source, maybe a baby on a piece of driftwood—what would we have done with such a thing? This ship was dangerous enough for an adult, let alone a child.

The Captain was pulling on his jacket over his nightshirt as he emerged. He peered straight ahead with his brass spyglass.

"Sirens," the Captain said simply.

"Like *The Odyssey*?" I asked. I had obviously heard tales (tails, tales, ha!) of such creatures but had believed it all to be myth. I should not have been surprised; on this journey, I've seen a great many impossible creatures. Why wouldn't there be some sort of fish-human hybrid?

"Don't be foolish, those don't exist," the Captain replied. "They're not magic."

"They're a type of fish," Wyatt told me in a hushed tone. He'd been much more solicitous after our adventure in the caves, more likely to answer my questions. He often dragged Scottie, Lindsay, and Mac to join Barlowe and me in the mess. He even offered to cut me into a game of poker which I declined. As you know, card games have never been my strong suit; I wear my emotions too clearly on my face.

"Are you saying that a fish is making that noise?" I asked.

He nodded and the Captain glared at us.

"Quiet as you can, tell everyone to prepare for sirens. Hopefully, they'll pass without noticing us, but we need to be prepared in case they do."

I did as I was told, even if I didn't quite understand, and even if —this will not surprise you—I secretly hoped that I would get to see the creature that had spawned the legends of mermaids. I need not have worried. As I walked from one end of the ship to the other, the crying intensified, causing the hull to tremble and reverberate. The ringing filled my mind, making it hard to hold on to thoughts. Before long, any alerts were unnecessary, Hobbs and Barnaby were tearing off strips of cotton and stuffing them in their ears, and by the time I found Joshua, he was already moulding little plugs of beeswax like sailors in *The Odyssey*.

I ran above deck with a set for the Captain.

I could see the sirens now, a swirling mass of large fish circling the boat just outside the range of our guns. Their faces were as pale as an English schoolboy's. Their mouths gaped with every cry, which resembled a sad wailing choir. Occasionally, one would let out a bone-chilling shriek that made me jump and all the hairs on my body stand on end. It was hard to tell how many there were as they swirled around the ship. Several dozen at least.

"What are they doing?" I shouted at Wyatt who leaned in.

"Hunting! They're trying to get us to jump in."

"Into the water?" He nodded. "Why would we do that?"

"It will make the noise stop," Barlowe said as he appeared at my side. He offered me a pair of earplugs he'd made himself, declaring that "the only thing Hobbs and Barnaby are good at making is trouble." I felt uncommonly flustered by Barlowe's attention, at him placing his ear so close to my mouth he nearly kissed the lobe. Mac teased me about it for the rest of the evening.

While Barlowe's earplugs blocked out most of the noise, as the evening progressed and the choir grew in intensity, I wondered how any of us would sleep. While at first I wondered why anyone would be tempted to throw themselves overboard to make it stop, I knew after a couple nights with no sleep, the crew might be overcome by the temptation of such extreme measures for a little bit of peace. By nightwatch, the sound felt like physical pressure; my skin hummed like the hull of the ship, a headache threw shadows across my vision.

When the sun rose, I could swear I heard words inside the screams, although I couldn't quite make them out and suspected they were a hallucination. How much longer until we were all hearing and seeing things that weren't there?

I served breakfast to a bleary-eyed crew.

Despite this, they worked hard that day in an attempt to speed up the ship and shake off our pursuers. But when the sun set, marking a full day of cacophony, they still had us surrounded, churning the water with the power of their song, rattling the ship and us with it. Their numbers seemed to have doubled as packs joined the initial scouts, drawn in no doubt by the sound, hoping they could feed off the scraps. Still, none moved in close enough for me to get a better look.

The next morning, I found Barlowe standing at the prow, holding nets, a spear discarded at his feet. He looked glum and exhausted. The tattoos on his arms seemed to quiver in frustration—a hallucination, surely.

"They keep moving out of my reach. We'll empty our ammo into the water before we manage to hit any of them."

"What can we do?"

"Hope they move on before we all lose our minds. Or something bigger comes to eat them but leaves us alone."

Tensions were high amongst the crew and a fight broke out over the good mop and the most comfortable privy seat. I bandaged up more cuts, scrapes, and bruises than usual. Tommy broke a second finger when a badly tied knot split and a pulley fell on his hand. He whined so loudly in the mess that Edric nearly clobbered him for disturbing his afternoon nap. He was normally such a quiet, sensible man, a good leader; to see him lash out like this should have been a sign he was about to snap.

It was dire. I was convinced I could hear my name in the sirens' wails. Everyone's throats were raw from shouting at one another, and more than one argument had broken out over a case of bad lip-reading. That afternoon, I had to stop Darby from pouring candle wax directly into his ears. I thought his actions overly rash at the time, but the same idea tempted me soon after.

As I was turning to supper preparations, a half-conscious Edric was dragged to the kitchen-hospital, babbling incoherently. His head and chest were soaking wet. Lindsay and Mac held onto him firmly, as if afraid he might run away. Turns out they were right to worry.

"We found him with his head in a bucket of water," Lindsay explained. He was the only one on the crew who seemed to be faring okay, likely because of his partial deafness.

I sat Edric down on the butcher's block. He was muttering and gazing into the middle distance even as I clapped in front of his face. The man was somewhere else entirely. I pulled the cotton from my ears only for the cacophony of the fish to batter me, my head pounding even harder than before. Even with the cotton out of my ears, I could only make out his words once I felt the warmth of his breath against my neck.

"Put me back, put me back, put me back."

He faced me, grabbing my cheeks. He was crying, snot rolling down his face.

"The song! It's so beautiful."

He stood up abruptly, shaking off the two men and pushing me down. He didn't check to see if his crew were okay; instead he sprinted out of the room. I shouted after him, shouted for others to stop him, but no one heard me. I pursued but only emerged onto the deck as he made it to the railing. Several others ran to intercept him, but no one managed to catch him before he leapt overboard.

As I peered over the railing, I saw the swirl of fish surrounding his body, pulling him down into the depths. The wailing cut off abruptly, replaced by Edric's gurgling screams.

"Get a net," I shouted at Barlowe, but he shook his head.

He likely thought I meant to try to rescue Edric, but even I knew that the nets would not support his weight. I was hoping to catch a specimen or two. The Captain rushed over to me, guessing at my purpose. I promised I'd keep it inside a barrel wrapped in old sails and in my room, but he glared at me until I decided not to press the issue.

I hope these notes will be enough evidence of this strange species and an explanation for the myth of the mermaid.

As I rest in the empty silence of the night, I wonder what Edric meant, that it sounded beautiful in the water? Was it just another hallucination caused by lack of sleep, or did the cries sound different with his head submerged? Perhaps he had not been trying to drown himself but to better listen to the fish that surrounded us.

I'll conduct experiments if I ever have the privilege to come across the species once more.

Yours,
Wilford

August 4th, 1760

ENTRY FROM JEAN BAPTISTE DE BEAUPRÉ'S JOURNAL

I SEEM to be haunted by memories of my dear Wilford. Even adverts in the paper remind me of him: "Mathy Marty, the horse of knowledge, a beast both wonderfull [sic] and strange". We'd seen a similar one ages ago: "Come see the Learned Pig perform feats of intelligence," which had us chuckling over breakfast. Then I saw Willie's eyes twinkle with mischief, and before I could point out we had a report due later that day, or that for the same price we could watch a play, he'd dragged me to the fair and got us seats in the front row of a raucous crowd. The "Learned Pig" stamped at the ground and snorted while the hog trainer told us how the sow could count, and even read thoughts.

Wil began asking a flurry of questions to the man and his porcine companion. What did the pig eat, what was her breeding stock, had he trained her from birth? Could she read or write? Solve mathematical problems? And while I know his sincere curiosity about the world… others seem to find this level of scrutiny condescending; the trainer did not take kindly to Wilford's questioning. He proposed a wager: "Ask how many are present, and if she answers true, you owe me a shilling. What say you?"

"I'd much rather ask her something specific," Willie countered. "How many fingers am I holding behind my back? Surely, if she can read minds, this would be easy."

Of course, having taken front row seats in Wilford's excitement to get close to the foul-smelling psychic pig, the majority of the crowd sat behind us in view of his slender fingers. I could see the redness rising in the trainer's cheeks as he realised he'd been outsmarted, and stifled a laugh.

Poor Wil was quite disappointed to find it was all a trick, likely brought on by the trainer's secret cues. I believe he was quite excited at the prospect of a conversation with an animal, even if I'd suspected it was nothing but a ruse. I pulled him away as the crowd began to demand a refund.

If only he were still here, I'm sure he'd drag me to meet Mathy Marty the Horse, hopeful that this time he might find a true animal prodigy.

Alone, I'd get no joy from the obvious dupe and be too self-conscious to ask the questions that would paint Mathy Marty's trainer as a fraud. In times like these, I am overcome with how much I miss Wil's cleverness and playfulness.

I wish there was something I could do to help him, to save him from the pirates. I wouldn't have the first clue how to find him or how to rescue him. Wil was always the one who took charge, who had the brilliant ideas, who brought me along for his escapades. Without him, I am faced with my own inability to act, my own ineptitude.

If I went, I'd just get us both in even greater trouble.

Perhaps there are some with the Navy or Royal Society who might be able to help.

August 7th, 1760

LETTER FROM WILFORD BOWEN TO JEAN BAPTISTE DE BEAUPRÉ

DEAREST JEAN —

Sorry for the delay once again. The last couple of days have been a flurry of activity followed by much-needed rest. I hadn't had much to report until yesterday.

After fleeing the sirens, we pushed to Santa Maria in Cape Verde to survey our hull for damage from their acoustic assault.

You should see these beaches! Nothing but clean white sand, and fish more colourful and plentiful than I ever thought possible! While we can't fish in the reefs due to superstition — Mac in particular is convinced that eating these fish will offend the gods who use the reefs as a home and cause them to curse us — there is plenty around the beaches for us to eat. And so many coconuts!

It had been a rather calm couple of days, with most of the crew cleaning the hull and patching up anything Wyatt and Scottie deemed worrisome. The men worked shirtless, displaying those strange circular bruises I still could not explain. Tommy and I were on fish-smoking and food preparation duty. Although I was doing most of the work on account of his two broken fingers, he kept me entertained by singing bawdy songs a child his age should never know. The work was nearly finished and we were enjoying a last day of fun in the sun. Despite spending their lives on the water, most of the men were rather reluctant to swim but were quite happy to practise hitting each other on the head with sticks while playing in the sand, Hobbs and Barnaby in particular. However, a great racket arose from down the beach.

A hundred birds calling at once.

I grew fearful that something in the woods had startled them, that some great predator we had not yet encountered was making itself known.

A shape emerged from the jungle, running quickly towards us. It took me a moment to realise it was Scottie and not some fearsome beast.

A shadow fell over him—the mass of swirling birds in the sky. They were all a vivid green; however, they seemed to vary a lot in morphology, some with large wings while others had prominent brightly coloured beaks. I was—and still am—unclear whether these were all different species working together or the same species where individuals had developed different traits. The dense mass whirled, taking the shape of a large bird. What was most astonishing was that each member of the flock flew in formation according to its exaggerated trait, thus those with large talons flew near the feet while the ones with large crests flew above the head. It was a creature of great internal harmony, a system where the strengths of each animal were used to the advantage of the group.

Barlowe pulled me into the huddled mass of the crew. I hadn't even noticed that I'd been so exposed.

The call changed, sharp and angry, like a parent warning you away from its nest.

"Prepare to fire!" the Captain shouted, and the men loaded their guns. "Fire!"

I wondered if this might be my chance to collect some specimens, but other than losing a few feathers, no bird was hit. Everyone reloaded as quickly as possible, but I could tell the birds were not too happy about the current predicament, those near the throat letting out ear-splitting calls while the central mass swirled with a renewed fervour that was dizzying to watch.

And Scottie was the closest thing on which to vent their frustration.

They dove, the birds making up the feet wrapping around him and pulling him into the air. The beak pecked Scottie, splitting his face open like a seed before tossing him down. He collapsed on his knees and fell forward in the sand. They continued to peck and tear at him, his body twitching under the force of their onslaught.

His blood coloured the white sand crimson.

The crew watched silently, stock still, until Wyatt let out a pained howl.

The bird mass let out a victorious cry in answer, and Wyatt surged forward, only to be stopped by Lindsay. He pulled Wyatt, sobbing, back into the crew's mass and motioned for me to assist. I had seen Wyatt and Scottie talking under the stars at night, watching them until they became nothing but distant dark smudges, finding it impossible to turn away. I thought Wyatt would soon be asking me to rid him of his "wife Deborah," having moved on to a flesh and blood companion.

~~Watching them had given me a peek at a kind of life I'd never thought possible.~~

"Move towards the trees for shelter," the Captain said, and I dragged Wyatt as we started a slow shuffle. Our movement caught the birds' attention, the head swivelling in our direction. It let out another alarm call and the bird took to the air, now flying towards us.

A cluster of red birds at the crest flapped in our direction, a kind of warning. Like a bully puffing out his chest. Its screams were strident, and the circle of us stumbled back under its noise, recalling the terror we had lived through with the sirens.

"Fire!" the Captain ordered. But, again, it essentially did nothing; only feathers fell in the sand. I was too busy holding back Wyatt to run out and get them.

The birds that made up the conglomerate's feet reached down

towards us. Their talons were enormous, almost comically large compared to their fist-sized bodies. One landed on Lindsay, digging into his right eye. Blood and a thick clear jelly started leaking down his face. Another scratched along Barlowe's cheek.

A set of three or four snakes sprang from seemingly nowhere, perhaps from burrows in the sand. They were the golden tone of tanned flesh, their scales outlined like a coloured etching. Curiously, their pupils were not slit like normal snakes but had startlingly iridescent purple irises. The snakes seemed unfazed by us, climbing our bodies like ladders to get at the birds overhead. One snake bit the bird clawing at Barlowe and another shot up, disappearing into the mass which swarmed like bees.

The birds started to fall, first some from the talons, and then the emerald crest, and finally, a beak fell and implanted itself in Joshua's shoulder.

Other birds flew down and collected their fallen comrades, flying them back into the jungle.

At some invisible signal, the remaining birds took off, scattering before heading to the trees. Defeated. The crew flopped onto the sand, bloodied, exhausted. Wyatt ran immediately to Scottie's corpse, and I followed him—although I knew there was little for me to do. His face had been completely smashed in, teeth, brains, and bones mixing in the bowl of his skull. I would never have been able to identify him from what remained of his face alone.

Wyatt pulled Scottie to his chest, cradling what was left of his head. I felt a pang that must have been the merest shadows of Wyatt's devastation. I'd known Scottie only a month but he'd been one of the men aboard I'd considered a friend. I wasn't quite sure what to say; it was clear Wyatt was grieving a lover. Luckily, Barlowe arrived with a flask of rum and an offer to give the man the protection and privacy he needed.

I set off to deal with the physical wounds I was more capable of tending.

While the crew dug Scottie's grave, I removed the snapped-off beak—the size of a thumbnail—from Joshua's shoulder and bandaged some cuts. Lindsay said he was happy it was his right eye since at least he can see out one side of his face and hear out the other. He insists the new patch makes him look fearsome.

We held a solemn funeral, Barlowe supporting Wyatt, who stared intently at Scottie while he was lowered into the hole, as if pleading for him to reveal it had all been an elaborate joke. We held him back when he tried to follow the corpse. The Captain did not tell Wyatt to pull himself together or admonish him when Wyatt slapped at him without much power or coordination. Instead he placed the shovel in Wyatt's hands and helped him bury his lover. We all watched in silence, and when the hole was filled, Wyatt collapsed onto the sand. Barlowe carried him back to the ship and to the "treasure room." I'm not quite sure when he will come out.

The *Goddess* pushed off as soon as the tide was high enough. We were eager to get away before the birds—or Bird—regrouped and tried to take their revenge.

I do wish I could have had a better look at it. Or had the presence of mind to collect the fallen feathers from the sand. I must have been more affected by the death than I initially realised to have neglected my scientific duties. In retrospect, I must say: it was quite a remarkable specimen!

A meta organism, all its parts working together to make a whole. One of the birds making up the feet would likely not have been able to tear apart its meal alone, needing those in the head area to assist. And vice versa. It was a truly startling example of the importance of community, of the varied roles of the different individuals. How together they are greater than the sum of their parts. And while I do have some feathers and the aforementioned beak, those components are hardly enough to capture the majesty of the organism. I'd need samples from the entire individual, some of the colourful crest, the talons, and the keen eyes.

I also neglected to search the beach for evidence of the snakes. I wonder at their provenance, how they hid so quickly after the struggle.

The other crew dodged my questions about the snakes. I wonder if it's the same kind of superstition Mac has about coral reefs.

We'll be heading to port soon and I'm hoping I'll find a way to send these letters. I hope you are also having your own adventures and thinking of me as often as I think of you.

I do not know that I'll ever find anything as marvellous on this earth as you, Jean.

Yours,
Wilford

August 8th, 1760

MY EXPERIMENTS AREN'T DOING WELL and neither is Willie's case.

I've been concentrating far too much on finding ways to bring Wilford home (or on all the ways he might be prevented from coming back, but I cannot dwell on these) that I've been neglectful of my studies. And now it seems I can't do either well.

I've tried contacting the Navy since they were the ones who lost him in the first place. Stands to reason they'd try to rescue one of their own who'd been kidnapped by pirates. The clerk said Wilford had "willingly boarded the pirate ship in the first place and done the dishonourable thing." According to him, if the Navy went out looking for Wilford, it would be as a criminal rather than a victim. He strongly recommended I drop my inquiry, even offered to do me a favour and burn the requisition.

"You've got a bright future. Better forget about him, for your own sake."

It took every ounce of self-control to not break his pompous beaky nose. Especially after he asked me whether I was free for a card game amongst "like-minded folks."

I then tried Wilford's parents and brothers. He'd often joked that, as the youngest of three, he was "the spare of the spare," and thus, his health and safety weren't a priority. I'd called him pessimistic, but I see now the truth of this statement.

They simply waved away my concerns. His father even called the kidnapping his son's "little ocean tour" as if he hoped that Wilford would be whisked away, never to return. They obviously saw no cause to worry and offered no help.

In a fit of desperation, I tried the Society.

I read them Wilford's letters, tried to convince them of the enormous scientific value of the findings, and that we should try to rescue him before all of his knowledge was lost in the event of his death. I was nearly laughed out of the assembly. They won't defend him because he isn't a Fellow, and according to them, these letters sound like "the ranting of a madman." I heard someone say he was happy to have been the one to turn down Wilford's application. Others I'd thought of as friends uttered the same warning as the Navy clerk, to keep quiet or my own reputation would be at stake.

Even my advisor, who I suspect knows of my feelings for Wilford because of his knowing smiles, advised me to move on. "This will end your career. It will destroy your life. No one will take this seriously, not without mountains of evidence and maybe not even then. But certainly, no one will fund an expedition to rescue someone they think is mad."

I had to leave before I started yelling.

What venues are left?

And when will I hear from him again?

I've always let Wilford take the first steps, do the hard thing. With him gone, there's no one left to save him. No one but me.

August 12th, 1760

LETTER FROM WILFORD BOWEN TO JEAN BAPTISTE DE BEAUPRÉ

Jean,

The nights have grown hotter, making it difficult to sleep through till morning. Not nearly as gloomy as dear old England! As of late, I wake naturally before dawn and take a stroll on the deck, chatting with whoever is on watch before starting my duties.

The sea was calm this morning. I stood on the forecastle gazing at the waves for several minutes before I realised Captain Samson was right behind me—the smoke from his pipe was downwind and for once I had not smelled his arrival. I asked if there was anything he needed from me and he shook his head, then leaned over the railing.

"You know, I wasn't always a pirate," he told me. "My mother died in childbirth—my life for hers. My father reminded me of it often." He rolled up his coat sleeve, showing me a series of small circular burns, then let out a strange barked laugh. "Cigars were his bedfellows. Snuffed them out on me.

"As soon as I could, I ran away. Thankfully, I found work. Able-bodied young men are always in demand on ships, as they tend to drop like flies. Sickness gets a lot of 'em. I became a cabin boy like our dear Tommy. I learned to help the cook with meals. I learned to fish, and folks were gladder for the extra supply. A full-bellied captain can win you a lot of favours. Once I proved I could be more than a runner, they taught me to handle ropes and knots, and before long I was up in the rigging like a proper sailor. That kind of foot-work lends well to swordsmanship, it turns out. It's a hard life, I admit that. But I treat my crew well. Men can turn just as quickly as the sea; you've got to know when to push back or hold firm. Even so, you'll find no whippings here." I recalled that, yes—I had never witnessed capital punishment during my time on the *Sea Goddess*. The threat of marooning was enough for some.

"My post was handed down to me by the previous Captain, a man named Neal. A gunshot wound in his leg went bad. No Doctor on the crew at that time, mind you." He took heavy pauses between these recollections. It was the most I've heard him speak. "I sat by his bedside in those final days. He knew of my upbringing. He told me … that our fathers do not make us men. Our conduct does. Told me I did good, that the *Goddess* would be in good hands."

He took a long puff from his pipe and exhaled towards the sky. "You're a queer fellow, I must admit." I watched him turn back to the cabin and stride away before he stopped. "But you're a good man."

As Mac emerged from below decks, passing the Captain with a jovial salute and giving me a wave, I was struck not just by the fact that the Captain had told me this personal tale, but also that I had somehow become friends with the crew. And while their eyes glaze over when I tell them about my latest scientific discoveries—unlike you, who always listened with interest—I know we'll fight together when danger arises.

I wish you were here to join us.

- Wil

August 22nd, 1760

ENTRY FROM JEAN BAPTISTE DE BEAUPRÉ'S JOURNAL

THE LAST FEW days have been quite hectic. Another packet of Wilford's letters arrived.

How can he face such terrors with the same childlike wonder of our youth? Sometimes I worry Wil has knocked something loose in his brain. *Giant worms? Sirens?* It's like a Greek legend. But he is no Hercules. Sooner or later he'll be hurt, or worse.

After my disastrous attempts to get help from my Fellows, I realised there is only one option.

If I want Willie rescued, I must do it myself.

It's not just the danger, although that's a big part of it. This growing kinship between him and the other men, the continued affections and care of Barlowe, makes me terrified of what this might mean for us. I know I should be happy that he is so well cared for, but I cannot help but feel that as our geographical distance grows, so too does our emotional connection. When will it break under the strain? When will he fall into Barlowe's strong arms and forget all about me?

I know my jealousy is not my greatest asset; neither is my "disaster thinking." But I do not want us to grow so far apart we can never again come back together.

I've sent notices to The Royal Society and my father's estate that I am taking a sabbatical to study silk in Lyon, that the stress of Wilford's departure has become too much and I plan to recuperate by the seaside. I told the same to my advisor but I do not believe he bought my lies. I'm not certain that my position will be waiting for me upon my return. But that is no longer my primary concern.

I'll be on my way to Bristol in the morning and will hopefully find a ship to take me to the West Indies shortly after. I cannot let myself think of all the ways this could go wrong (fire in the engine, robbers on the train, a bridge collapse).

Getting there will be the easy part. The hard part will be finding him.

August 23rd, 1760

LETTER FROM WILFORD BOWEN TO JEAN BAPTISTE DE BEAUPRÉ

MY DEAREST FRIEND,

I find myself lost for words, struggling with where to begin — I'm sure you will find that very amusing, as I can readily admit I have always been quite the prater. But this, I'm afraid, escapes even my vocabulary. What I witnessed late last night, or rather early this morning, goes beyond the realm of what I deemed scientifically possible. I know that may seem like an exaggeration, considering my previous descriptions of fantastical and ferocious beasts. I've never been quite as affected… both physically and mentally, by one, though. Moreover, if the crew were to discover this letter and its contents, they would most certainly kill me. A small blessing that most cannot read, then.

My apologies, dear Jean-Baptiste. I promise every word is true.

I have begun to truly enjoy my time on the ship. I have even begun to join the crews' nightcaps, on occasion, although I cannot hope to match their level of revelry. In fact, they find it quite amusing how quickly I reach my limit, calling me a lightweight. After our incident with the birds, and during one of these drinking sessions, the Captain declared to the crew that I had finally gained my sea legs and was ready to meet "Her." Unlike their usual raucous portance, the men became solemn, reverent. This should have tipped me off that something was amiss, but I was "three sheets to the wind," as they say.

The next day after sword practice, Barlowe clapped me enthusiastically on the shoulder, grinned, and commended me. Asked if I was "ready to meet the Goddess?" I smiled back—unsure of what to say—and responded affirmatively, telling the man that I was honoured. I'm afraid my proclivity for proper decorum is ingrained into my very soul. It is both a blessing and a curse, as you well know.

After a hearty dinner, Barlowe instructed Tommy to finish cleaning while he led me to a room that I'd previously been barred access to: the treasure room. Wyatt had emerged bleary-eyed from it just yesterday, seemingly a bit better but not the raucous man I had come to call a friend.

Barlowe told me that what lay within was sacred, and aside from his regular duties, he was charged with "Her" care. His eyes glinted as he told me this, and he had a kind of hunger in him that spoke of something that couldn't be satisfied by a meal.

He was also charged with barring new crew members from entering until they were deemed trustworthy. The Captain had granted me an "audience" with Her and, depending on my conduct, would see about future visits. My stomach was tied in knots. After knocking and announcing ourselves, the door opened.

Barlowe stepped forward and sunk to his knees, my presence completely forgotten, in front of a gargantuan mound of flesh as tall as a horse, roiling folds contorting and seeping a clear liquid, with large cerulean veins pulsing throughout. The jellyfish-like beast with a collection of arms—some of which resembled the suckered arms of an octopus while others were frilled and delicate—was set into an enormous, shallow trough filled with several inches of water, and with each movement, the basin sloshed its contents on the floor. The wetness washed over my boots.

I saw the resemblance* with the figurehead at the front of the ship, crude as it was.

An acidic odour assaulted my senses and stung my nostrils. The entire room was humid, causing me to break out in a sweat. Before me was a vivid, shocking sky-blue creature with yellow dots throughout—like a bird of paradise or tropical fish. Under the torch-light, the surface shimmered with an alluring luminescence, dancing across the beast. Looking at it too long made my head feel fuzzy. I am not sure which end was the head or the rear.

A handful of the crew pushed in behind me, nearly knocking me over. They acted as if in a trance, shucking their clothing into a pile near the doorway. Huxley was among them. I called out to him, but he did not answer. Likewise, they prostrated before the beast, and after what I can only describe as a prayer, split up and took "positions" down the length of the basin. Hobbs and Barnaby were there too—mirror images of each other, one on my left and right. I couldn't tell who was who from the backside.

Large tentacles sprung from the underside of the creature, probing the air and floor around us, easily twice the length of my body. The twins and Huxley, completely nude, grappled with these appendages. I blinked to clear my eyes and realised each was... pleasuring themselves, with this *thing*. Tendrils wrapped around their bodies, their faces flush in ecstasy.

How had the crew brought this aboard? How long had it been trapped here? I apologise. These questions haunt my waking thoughts, for I will never know the answers. As much as it pains the logical side of me, I cannot bring myself to ask—some innate chain binds me. Perhaps a side effect of my proximity.

Then Barlowe joined them, his face pressed against the mass... he was professing his love for the "Goddess" and thanking Her for the blessings She gave to the crew. I saw him shudder and could see a tentacle working down his throat. Another wrapped around his leg and inched towards his buttocks. Although I looked away, I could guess its intention. The snake tattoos on his arms moved, slithering circles up and down his skin. A wave of recognition washed over me

—these were the snakes I saw on the beach on the day of the bird attack! Were these the blessings he spoke of?

The air felt thick and heavy. I believe this creature was giving off some sort of pheromones—for some reason, I was unaffected. The crew were drawn like cattle to feed, yet I felt no desire to interact with her at all—quite the opposite.

But then another strange feeling came over me.

I cannot lie to you—seeing the men like that was overwhelming. It wasn't the Goddess that enraptured me; it was imagining you, like Barlowe, in those same throes of passion. Hearing their moans and seeing the sway of their backs filled me with fire. Something inside me felt like it was waking up. I thought of you and that night with the absinthe... and many things beyond. The way your forehead creases just so when you concentrate. How you lick your fingers before turning the pages of a book. Things I've absorbed dozens of times catapulted to the forefront of my mind, my thoughts repeating *Jean, Jean, Jean...*

After watching for several minutes I could stand it no longer and returned to my quarters.

I am slightly ashamed of what I did next. You deserve better than to have someone like me sullying your visage with these impure thoughts. My conscience could not hide this from you either, though. Please forgive me.

At breakfast the next morning, the few who had visited the Goddess were in extremely high spirits. Barlowe asked me if I enjoyed myself—evidently, he failed to notice my premature departure. I asserted I had, and prattled off some praise. Satisfied, he turned to leave and I noticed several new circular marks adorning his body. Huxley had a prominent one on his neck as well, a parting gift from their benefactor. I could finally explain the bruises I saw on the crew during their medical examinations.

I must admit, I am quite shaken by what I've discovered about myself. By the realisation of what you mean to me, by how you've always been more than just a friend, regardless of what I told myself.

But I'm also shocked by my lack of desire for the Goddess. The crew's worship of Her was more than just carnal pleasure; it was general affection, the way they spoke. It was love, just a peculiar one. One I do not share.

I will need to come up with a suitable excuse to turn down future invitations to the bacchanalia.

I have to wonder—did I make a mistake, coming here? I am becoming more and more unsure of how I will return home. Captain Samson seems quite attached to me and my "talents." Will I ever see you again, dear Jean? Are you just the same as when I left? I imagine you lounging in your favourite nook, a cup of Earl Grey, the morning sun competing with your equally radiant smile.

I hope to see that sight again.

-W

August 23rd, 1760

ENTRY FROM JEAN BAPTISTE DE BEAUPRÉ'S JOURNAL

ONCE MY TRAIN tickets were secured, the rest of the journey went without a hitch, none of my worst-case scenarios coming true. I tried not to chide myself on the way to the seaside for having delayed my rescue mission out of what I now realised was irrational fear.

My intention was to find the first vessel sailing across the Atlantic, money be damned. I've never been a lavish spender, and with no vices to speak of, my pockets were far from empty. Mid-afternoon, the docks were unsurprisingly busy with a flurry of activity and barked orders intertwining on the salt air. As I wandered through the sailors and travellers, I spotted a very tall, broad man holding a sign. He wasn't advertising goods or preaching to passers-by. Simply standing and waiting.

His sign read "Jean."

I truly believe Wilford was giving me a swift kick in the rear, spurring me to action, as I can find no logical reason why I approached the gentleman. There was no possible way he meant me! These things just do not happen.

"You're waiting for someone named Jean?" I asked nervously.

He looked down at me (from at least six inches above my own height) and smiled.

"Are you the Frenchman? Jhee-on?" His accent was strange. I couldn't place it.

Fear would hold me back no longer. "Yes."

"My name is Da'mon. I come to you as an envoy of the Tear." He bowed slightly and placed a hand over his chest. A large tattoo, a dark outline of an eye, covered the back of his palm. It looked like it might come alive and blink at me. I tried not to look at it in case it did. "You are looking for the man called WB?"

"Do you mean Wilford?"

"Yes—that is it. The Tear's messages are not always perfect. We do our best to interpret."

"I'm not sure if I follow you."

"All will be explained in time. I am sure you can understand the need for secrets. Collect your luggage and meet me here in one hour."

The idea I would obey was ridiculous. Even now after having come all this way, conquering my fear, I found it creeping back. Following a strange man who knew my name *and* Wilford's could very well be a trap, either some humiliation devised by the Fellows or my father aiming to teach me a lesson. But there was something of the man that had the same magic I found in Wilford's letters. Following him felt like just the thing Wilford would do—and if I had any hope of finding my dearest friend, surely doing as he would was my best bet. I had to be strong for him.

When I returned, bags in tow, we set out on a small rowboat and paddled a fair distance from the port where a large ship was waiting behind the cliff face. Painted a deep, rich red, it was armed with three cannons on each side. I made sure to get a good look at the figurehead, thinking back on the *Sea Goddess* my Wilford told me about, what feels like so long ago. This one bore a mermaid with hands holding out a large polished orb. I could have sworn it was a giant pearl, but that was impossible. Painted to resemble one, more likely.

I was hoisted onboard and greeted by a striking figure, a black man with a dark blue coat and a hard-set face. He greeted me in French.

"I apologise—I'm afraid we're not a welcome sight in England. We don't come this far east very often, to be honest, but these are special circumstances. My name is Tiberius, and I am the Captain of the *Watchman's Favour*. We've been tasked to escort you to WB. There are signs of danger in his future—a threat to life and Gods alike—which we must prevent."

I shook his hand and asked him a flurry of questions that would have impressed Wil. How did he know I was searching for Wilford? How did they know I'd be at the dock? Did they know where he was, and how to find him? What danger? His answers just opened more questions. Finally… what was this Tear? He laughed at me and simply pointed up.

I have no idea how I missed it before. Up above the sails, positioned where the crow's nest would normally be, was a large circular metal cradle resting on a platform. A man sat on the edge near it, wielding a large spear. Inside sat a spiny mass covered in eyes— thousands of eyes—like a sea urchin made from overlapping oculi. It shifted, and I felt it looking at me, looking through me, but strangely, it felt … comforting. Like a parent peeking through a cracked door to watch over their sleeping child.

Captain Tiberius also had an eye tattoo on his hand—and in fact, all the crew did. "We are envoys of the Tear," he explained. "It sees through us, and we carry out its will."

"And this Tear … told you about Wilford?"

He explained they knew where he was last week, or nearabouts. A map had been laid out in the Captain's quarters with small figures placed in different regions. He pointed to one that looked like a squid and said that was Wilford and his crew. An eye represented Tiberius and his men. The Tear would send out some sort of signal, and whatever came back, they would record and interpret. Sometimes it got muddled, Tiberius said. Something to do with the distance, or difficulty of the task? No one was exactly sure. I felt like I was back at Oxford with the professors lecturing for hours on end on subjects I had no understanding of.

Before I knew it, night had fallen. My luggage had been placed in a small cabin complete with a desk for writing. Someone even left me a nice woollen blanket, folded on the corner of my small cot. I couldn't watch our departure from port; it was suddenly too real that I had left the security and safety of land and placed my trust in a group of strangers — pirates, no less. It's too late now to go back.

Da'mon brought me a tray of supper when he noticed my absence at the mess. When I could not bear to swallow even the smallest bite, he offered me some of the foul green liquid that got me into this predicament. I turned him down.

The Captain stopped by later to see how I was doing. He refused my — handsome — payment for passage, reiterating this was all part of their duty.

They told me it was *my* duty to save Willie.

August 24th, 1760

LETTER FROM WILFORD BOWEN TO JEAN BAPTISTE DE BEAUPRÉ

DEAREST JEAN,

What a week it's been aboard the *Goddess*. Whenever I see the masthead, I can't help but recall what I witnessed below. It's strange to think She's been on the ship this entire time and how this thought does not excite me as it does the other men. I should be entranced by Her, yet for all the pleasure She supposedly brings, I only feel wonderment at my proximity to a scientific curiosity.

Despite my earlier fears, I have found myself quite adept at making up excuses when others offer to accompany me to the "treasure room." It seems everyone is quite convinced with my bluff, although they've asked me to make these recipes I've claimed to be "researching." I'll need to come up with another lie soon.

I've been trying to keep up appearances, acting as my usual jovial self, but Wyatt noticed something was wrong. I was surprised to see him entering my kitchen as I was cleaning up after lunch. He did not usually offer to do the dishes, but since Tommy had suddenly disappeared again, I was happy for the help.

"We were all wondering when the Captain was going to introduce you to our Lady."

"Was I the only one who hadn't met her yet? Scottie and the others came on board after me."

I felt bad mentioning his former—friend? Lover? I had evidence it was the latter, but hadn't yet had the nerve to ask. Perhaps they were simply very close friends like you and I. I cannot even think of you dying without my stomach dropping like a ship on stormy seas.

"Yes, he'd visited Her several times. Scottie also did not find the Lady to his taste, nor any other woman. We've had several other crewmates throughout the years that have felt the same way, but most, like me, find Her company pleasurable even if they might find a male God just as, or more, entrancing. Or a God that's neither one or the other, or both."

He paused, staring at me rather pointedly. I knew what he was saying, but he was too polite to push the thread further.

"You know, the Goddess does not only offer physical pleasure and comfort. She can bestow other gifts."

He set aside the plate he had been washing to remove his shirt. I looked away, suddenly unsure of what he was going to do. I had seen his bare chest on many occasions in a medical capacity. But this felt different. He let out a chuckle at my bashfulness.

"Hello," came a high voice, feminine, something I hadn't heard in quite a while.

Curiosity outweighed the shameful tangle in my belly, and I turned to see Wyatt with his arm lifted to display the giant mole named Deborah on his side. For the first time, I could see what looked like features in the face-sized dark patch—a small dainty upturned nose any woman of society would have admired, and full round lips.

I am almost embarrassed to say I nearly fainted when she opened her eyes. They were a shocking violet.

Wyatt caught my arm before I could flee.

"Listen to what she has to say." He sat me down so that I was level with his wife's face. I no longer wondered if it was a joke.

"He'd warned me you might react this way, but I insisted on talking to you."

I believe I mostly uttered words of assent, but if I'm being frank, the conversation consisted mainly of me asking her about her bodily needs (she did not need sustenance, borrowing instead from Wyatt, but was quite capable of independent thought, and the two apparently often bickered about everything from clothing options to dietary choices, although both had loved Scottie in their own way).

But eventually, she grew solemn and what she said next will stay in my mind until my dying day.

She told me I was approaching a crossroads in my life. "Cowards die many deaths, dear Wilford. You'll have to stop running eventually. But which direction you turn next, that's just as important. Think with your heart." When I asked for more details, Deborah told me I'd have to figure it out myself, which confounded me and made Wyatt laugh.

I sat in shock for the rest of the afternoon, trying to make sense of what I had been told. I performed my medical duties numbly. It wasn't until the next day that I started to wonder, if Barlowe's strange tattoos and Wyatt's prophetic mole were gifts bestowed by the Goddess, what skills might the rest of the crew possess?

I turned to Tommy—where did he come from?—who was busy preparing new bandages, and asked him if he'd met Wyatt's wife. I'm sure I sounded quite flustered as I recounted my meeting with Deborah while working up the courage to ask him if there was anything he could do, if the Goddess had bestowed Her gifts on him as well. He laughed, gave a little shiver, and then faded from sight.

Camouflage! Human camouflage!

He reappeared with a beaming grin.

"Does everyone possess such talents? Have I been blind to them this whole time?" I asked.

"Not all of us," he said, "but most."

He told me that Mac could use his arm—that is, the one without the hook—to carry extremely heavy objects, far above a normal man's capacity, and offered with excitement to get me a demonstration tonight. Edric (may he rest in peace) could change seawater into fresh water by dipping his fingers in it. All skills that would be helpful at sea.

I wonder how soon they develop—might I have some hidden power as well?

Rationally, I do not understand how the crew can perform such feats, but it's clear just how little of the world the scientific community knows. The stuffy old Fellows at the Royal Society (excluding you, of course), whom I used to so greatly admire, could never even conceive of the things I've seen in my travels. Their model of the world is fundamentally flawed, and I can't help but feel a bit of pride for having seen some deeper truth in it.

When you read these tales from the comfort of normal old England, do you side with the Fellows and think me mad, or do you wish you were travelling by my side, seeing these same things?

Wilford

August 25th, 1760

LETTER FROM WILFORD BOWEN TO JEAN BAPTISTE DE BEAUPRÉ

DEAREST JEAN,

Please excuse the worse-than-usual penmanship. I am writing this onboard a crowded raft. The reason for that will become evident soon enough.

Do you remember when we went to Brighton and found those hermit crabs with such misshapen strange shells, like a whole colony of misfits? It was what inspired my thesis… the one that was insufficient in granting me entry into the Royal Society. I was so fascinated by their conglomeration of colours. These creatures would choose their own homes, their own vestments. I could not help but think about the way we humans do that too.

I wondered to what extremes they could go, what strange clothes or armaments they might be able to don. In a rare silly mood, you'd offered up one of your fancy shoes for their consideration only to be rather cruelly snubbed (and pinched in the toe, no less!)

Well, I was asking the right questions on that day because I've just met the most extraordinary hermit crab, one capable of feats I could have never imagined! And in spite of everything, I can't help but feel happy to have made its acquaintance.

We'd been sailing towards a chain of islands when we spotted *The Fate of the Unlucky.* The smaller ship was seemingly deserted, moored but listing. The Captain was called to decide our course of action: rescue or abandonment. There was bad blood between the two crews over a tincture the *Unlucky's* doctor had sold our First Mate. It turned his privates dark blue, repulsing the Goddess for a full moon cycle, and so there was a contingent that believed they deserved to stay marooned as retribution for their practical joke.

On our approach, we observed no movement on deck. It was listing hard on the starboard side, thus making it clear that the ship had likely been abandoned. It was free for plundering! Or so we thought.

"They have the prettiest cannons on that ship," Barlowe sighed, with stars in his eyes.

"If I remember correctly, while their doc wasn't too skilled at doctorin', he did have quite the collection of recipes," Mac chimed in, punctuating his statement with a jab to my ribs.

It was decided. We'd be the carrion of the sea.

We proceeded towards the *Unlucky* cautiously, loading a rowboat for the boarding party. I was, as usual, deemed too important to be sent on any adventures. (The Captain thought there was a possibility that the crew of the *Unlucky* were lying in wait to ambush any good Samaritans or wily thieves that might investigate.) Hobbs, Barnaby, and Huxley were lowered down along with guns and swords.

Barlowe prepared the cannons in case they were necessary and the skiff took off. The hulking twins moved the small craft at a speed that seemed inhuman. They crossed over the halfway point in the amount of time I would have spent fumbling with the paddles.

When nothing happened, I was about ready to relax in the sun and start writing you a letter, but suddenly the *Unlucky* shifted, correcting its list, sails audibly groaning at the abrupt movement.

The ship was not abandoned. This was indeed an ambush!

"Fire!" The Captain shouted. Barlowe obeyed.

His shots were true but the *Unlucky* moved faster than any ship

I'd ever seen, turning perpendicular to us so that while the cannon-ball should have hit the flank, it sailed along the side and plopped into the water.

A gasp arose along the deck as we saw what now occupied the masthead of the boat.

Perhaps you are unsurprised, considering how this letter began, but I found myself quite shocked to see an enormous hermit crab which had outgrown the shells of other marine creatures, instead housing its body within the confines of a rather unusual home—the *Unlucky*.

I guess the ship lived up to its nickname.

Its two massive asymmetrical claws reached towards us in fury! Its larger claw was bigger than the boarding ship in which Hobbs, Barnaby, and Huxley sat gazing at the beast, stunned. The smaller claw was around the size of Barlowe (so, still quite big!), covered in long red spines that gave it the look of a mace.

The crab snapped the large claw, the noise as loud as a cannon, and turned its stalked eyes on us.

I could see a hole in the port side of the ship through which its body was squeezed. I yearn to observe the vessel's interior, how the crab's body might have twisted through the tight spaces therein. I was prevented from closer observation by my lack of telescope and by Mac pulling me back with his hook.

At first, it seemed the crab was too focused on the *Goddess* to notice the small vessel heading its way, but the rowboat's sudden movement caught its attention. Why focus on the larger armed ship when it had an easy snack nearby?

Barlowe fired the cannons again, creating a gash on the port side that bled wood chips but nothing else. The shot did not hit anything vital, angering but not injuring the crab. Luckily for those on the unprotected boat, it turned away to charge us.

"Guns!" shouted the Captain, and men lined up at the starboard side, muskets lifted to their shoulders.

The scale of the crab hit me as it closed the distance. Its eyes were the size of cannonballs, black and full of fury. It clicked its claws again. That time, the sound wave ruffled the hairs on my head.

"Fire!"

Smoke and gunpowder filled the air as the guns erupted around me. The ship rocked under the blast of the cannons. The crab screeched, a high-pitched sound that could have broken glass, and I thought for one moment that it might have been vanquished — surely this was its dying cry. But it dispersed the smoke with a wave of its claw before bringing the same appendage down against the port side of the boat, gouging the balustrade and crunching the wood as it drew down through the deck and into the lower levels. I got as close to the crab as I could, holding the ropes as the ship rocked below my feet. Hands pulled me back as the claw smashed the deck once more, destroying the wood upon which I'd stood moments ago.

"Be careful," Lindsay said before sprinting off.

Wyatt ran off to survey the damage. I could already guess what he would find; we were taking on water. Perhaps I had been on the ship long enough to sense a shift in how she bobbed, or the Goddess Herself was making me perceive the harm that had come to Her home. My home too, I supposed. Although that realisation came too late.

I ran towards the deafening screams, knowing someone required my attention. The change in list of the *Goddess* had knocked Joshua from his perch and onto the deck. The crab seized this opportunity and dug its mace-like claw into his shoulder, dragging him towards its maw. I did not hesitate or think of my own safety. I lept on his torso, pinning him to the deck. We were still for a moment before sliding forward.

My weight alone wouldn't be enough to free Joshua.

Lindsay noticed our struggle and brought his cleaver down on the creature's arm, severing the claw. Joshua screamed as we landed roughly on the deck.

Tommy suddenly appeared holding my bag of supplies before vanishing into the fog. I'm glad he can hide — although that wouldn't serve him if the ship sunk. I tried to warn him but did not know in which direction to shout.

Looking at Joshua, I knew I was unlikely to be of much help.

The spikes had pierced all through his shoulder, tearing at the skin and muscle where we had tried to pull him free. And his legs had been badly broken from the fall. I knew, even in calm seas, I would be unable to salvage his arm or legs. He'd no longer be able to stand on the topmast, hair blowing in the wind, like some sort of thrill-seeking goat. I did the best I could, bandaging him up tightly and giving him as much laudanum as I could spare — dribbling some down his front as the ship jerked below us. It was as much to comfort me as it was to him. I had been doctoring long enough to know it was no use. I tried to find him a place off to the side where he was not in danger of being trampled underfoot by the crew running around us, firing guns, cannons and harpoons.

After returning his weak smile, I turned back to the fight. Even with one claw, the crab was destroying the ship. We were tipping hard portside. I stumbled forward, slipping on Joshua's blood.

These attacks were not random — the crab was focused on one specific spot.

The Goddess!

Realising the threat at the same moment, the Captain yelled, "Save Her! Someone protect Her!"

The crew became frantic once they realised it was not just their own lives at stake.

That's when I saw Hobbs and Barnaby climbing up the *Unlucky* atop the crab's back.

I saw them both salute the Captain and then hug one another. Then they did something quite remarkable, quite strange. Both men started to puke. As soon as the bile hit the skin of the crab, it started to burn and fizzle. The shell cracked, pieces falling into the beast's guts as easily as sugar dissolving.

Barlowe later told me that Barnaby could vomit an acidic slurry that ate away at most materials while his mirror image twin could spit out a basic solution that could dissolve matter just the same. According to the principles of chemistry, they would have cancelled one another out had they spat at the same place, but they kept their streams separate, dissolving the crab's unprotected skin in the process. I had heard of certain insects capable of this, but to see a human producing such a thing was extraordinary. Had the Goddess given them entirely new organs which created these fluids? Sadly, I will never know.

Under their assault, the carapace crumbled, its colourful organs revealed as the surrounding flesh melted away.

A cheer went up on board, but they celebrated too soon. The crab reached back blindly and caught Hobbs, snapping him in half with his claw. Barnaby screamed for his brother, plunging his hands into the exposed core of the crab, pulling out organs that were soft as porridge, and punching what he couldn't loosen.

"Jump!" Barlowe shouted at Barnaby. From this close, there was no doubt we could finish off the crab with one well-aimed cannonball. But then it reached back and grabbed the remaining twin, bringing him to his mouth before biting into his midsection. A reservoir of acidic slurry popped like an overfull cherry at the pressure, melting the crab's mandibles and splattering into its eyes. The stench of cooked seafood hit me again, reminding me of the slime mould-infested lobsters from months ago. It dropped Barnaby into the sea before throwing back its head in pain.

Our Master gunner took his shot and it landed true, going straight through the head and plunging into the soft, exposed entrails.

The sky rained viscera. Bits of crab landed in my hair as we rounded up the crew.

Wyatt appeared (I was relieved to see he had been relatively unscathed, only needing me to bandage up a couple of cuts and pull out some splinters) with several others who were pulling the Goddess up from below. They'd put Her into the biggest barrel they could find, so large it took two men to wrap their arms around and lift it, and still one or two of Her tentacles draped over the side. She projected an air of unease—standing completely still unlike the gentle sway I'd observed in the treasure room—as if Her current accommodations were below Her standards.

"Nothing we can do. The ship is going to sink," Wyatt told the Captain.

We gathered what supplies we could, hurriedly building some

rafts. The Goddess was the first onboard, the crew would have it no other way.

I felt an unexpected wave of sadness as the masts of the *Sea Goddess* sank below the waves. It had been my home for months now, and even with the awkwardness of the last week, I found that I had grown to love it. And when I fought alongside the crew, I realised that, strangeness with the Goddess aside, they were the closest things to friends I had perhaps ever had—other than you, of course. I sang along as best I could to the funeral dirge for our three fallen mates and let myself be held as we shared our stories.

I was happy I'd tucked my letters into my bag for safekeeping, and other than being a little waterlogged from the transfer to the raft, they were all intact. I looked over at Barlowe, who had laid a protective hand upon the Goddess. We shared exhausted smiles.

We found Huxley holding onto the oars and some bits of wood and pulled him onboard. Now we're setting off again. The crew says there's a port nearby, Tortuga, which is supposed to be a pirate haven. I only hope we find shelter before we run out of supplies.

Yours,
WB

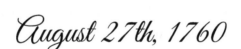
August 27th, 1760

ENTRY FROM JEAN BAPTISTE DE BEAUPRÉ'S JOURNAL

TODAY WAS my first day doing "caretaker duty", a task all crew members are required to perform once a fortnight. As I am the newest "recruit," I was under the supervision of an older crew member named Stanley, who has quite an impressive display of scars covering his body, including a web-like pattern on his bald head.

I am taken aback by the level of both cleanliness and professionalism among Tiberius's crew—are these truly pirates, or something else entirely? The main deck is quite large, maybe ten to fifteen metres in length, and the crew is constantly busy, their movements graceful, synchronous as if choreographed. My presence did not seem to disturb their rhythm; they simply sidestepped around me when I was in the way. As I waited for Stanley by the main mast, I watched a man lean on the railing, his hand covering an eye as he looked out to the horizon. He stood like this for a moment before nodding and heading off towards the Captain's quarters. Perhaps it helped him see better? Undoubtedly they've discovered some tricks for dealing with the sun's harsh rays.

My trepidation held me back less and less the longer I spent at sea, and I found myself excited rather than afraid about the prospect of getting close to The Tear for the first time—even with that daunting climb. The fifty-foot mast was equipped with a simple set of rungs, making the climb easier, even if the wind pulled at me more strongly with every step.

Once situated at our post, I was overwhelmed with the sheer force of The Tear's gaze—it felt like a pair of hands trying to grab me, and I had to hold on to the mast to steady myself. Stanley let out a bark of laughter and advised me not to fall.

At this distance, I'd say the creature was the size of a horse-drawn carriage, although not nearly as uniform in shape. Hundreds—nay, thousands—of eyes, from tiny pinpricks to saucers, with different colours and iris shapes, turned to peer at me at once. Even those on the backside of the creature—I'm not sure how I knew that; I just felt it.

Not a single eye was like the others, as if each had been plucked from some different exotic creature and added to this dragon's hoard. Some of them stood still, unblinking, while others were constantly moving, this way and that. There was intelligence in them, something bottomless I could not hope to comprehend.

I tried to ask about its origins, how it came to be on the ship, how it was fitted into the cradle, but unfortunately I received only shrugs and "it's always been here." I wonder if, underneath that mass, it has an underside like a snail or suction cups? Maybe it crawled up here itself? I can't imagine a crew hoisting it up here. Where did it live before coming on the ship?

Under the hot sun we doused The Tear in water and cleaned a heavy yellow mush from the corners of its many eyes, like dust caught from a night's sleep. I stared into a large dark iris for what seemed like hours, the black spot tunnelling backwards, stars glittering in the void. I was roused with a gentle shake. I'd been nearly tipping over the edge, fingers losing their grip on the mast. "Don't get lost in there," Stanley told me.

I know with my mission to rescue Wilford, I cannot lose myself in the possibilities the Tear presents to me, but I can still find myself drawn into its uncanny current. What would Wil make of this

strange creature? I imagine he'd try to seek out some natural explanation, or blame my dreams and hallucinations on the sun or my
"weak constitution." But I don't want to reduce these experiences to
something so banal. I find myself intrigued by these phenomena in a
way I have not felt in ages.

As I settled in for bed that night I felt a strange tingling pain in
my hand, akin to a bee sting after the initial pain had lessened.
Perhaps the creature stung me. Or, perhaps I have been writing too
much.

August 29th, 1760

LETTER FROM WILFORD BOWEN TO JEAN BAPTISTE DE
BEAUPRÉ

JEAN—

I don't have much time. The next ship north leaves in an hour, so
I'll need to write quickly if I have any hope of sending you this final
message.

We arrived in Tortuga two days ago, under the cover of nightfall.
And thank the Goddess we did. Our rafts were cramped and smelled
twice as bad as you can imagine—a half dozen men sitting knee to
knee for two days! The Goddess was thankfully unharmed and
swam alongside our rafts and rowboat. She was majestic to watch,
Her long sinuous body, the graceful way She glided alongside us.
Cramped inside the ship, I'd had no true understanding of Her size
and strength until then. I found it comforting to see Her following
us, watching over us still, although Barlowe feared for Her any time
She dove out of sight.

When we made it to port, we had to figure out how to get Her on
land (we couldn't leave Her unprotected in the water). We loaded
Her and some seawater into the rowboat and covered it with tarps to

keep Her from the prying eyes of common folk while we found a place to shelter. I remember my own shock upon seeing Her for the first time and can only imagine the city-wide panic that would occur were She spotted by the uninitiated!

The port town was not as lively as the crew had made it out to be on the journey here. I thought at first this was because I'd lived in London my whole life and was used to much more bustle, but I soon learned there were other reasons for the town's gloomy mood. We were watched with interest by those in the town, several approaching us to inquire whether we had arrived by ship and whether we had space for passengers. They wandered off when they learned that the rowboat was all we had for transport.

As we moved away from port, the sailors and merchants made way for families.

We laid low in a long-abandoned storehouse while we found our land legs. There were a couple of dwellings nearby out of which emerged some dirt-covered children. Barlowe tried to scare them away, lest they discover our Goddess. We covered the windows with our sails to keep out their prying eyes.

Our intent was to purchase a new ship and make the necessary adjustments to house Her in its embrace. When I asked how we'd acquire the funds for such an endeavour, as the vast majority of our valuables had been lost, the Captain responded, "The Goddess provides." The mutually beneficial relationship between Her and these men is endlessly fascinating and equally strange.

Regardless, we will be grounded here for several weeks, at least.

The Captain announced on the first morning that he had business to attend to and promptly disappeared. Barlowe headed the crew, guarding the Goddess day and night, while others searched for temporary employment or drink/gambling establishments. Only one was found, the Boot and Heel tavern. Surprisingly, many businesses and homes had been shuttered, although I did not understand why at the time. But I felt this matched the sombre tone of the town. However, due to its—dare I say skilled—cook, my own cooking duties were diminished.

"Finally, some good food," Mac said. The cheek!

As for the medicinal side of things, everyone had been patched up from the incident with the crab so, aside from regular bandage changing, I had plenty of free time. I started rewriting my more waterlogged notes.

Late that first night, a man burst through the doors at the Boot and Heel tavern, his voice hoarse from screaming. He'd heard of our arrival and had searched everywhere for us. The crew looked my way and I took a swig of draught before following the poor man, named George, back to his residence.

The couple lived near the edge of the village, and as we hurried to his wife's aid, passersby gave us strange, solemn looks and whispered to each other.

"Is it infectious?" I asked him.

"In a sense," he replied—which did not reassure me.

George explained the town was the victim of a demonic entity. Although there were no detectable changes in behaviour or memory while victims were possessed, once released from the parasite, the afflicted would decline within hours, the former shell scooped clean. The length of possession was never the same, although younger victims on average lasted longer. All times of infection were just guesses based on when the previous victim died, but it was easy to tell when the parasite vacated its host. Their skin would become loose and grey, and their muscles spasmed and jerked unnaturally. They would lose the ability to eat or drink, gradually becoming weaker until they were taken from the world. George described it as if one aged backwards; his wife became a baby in an adult's body.

It had killed a dozen locals in the past fortnight.

This evil spirit had come to be known as the Skin Dweller—a name that sends chills down my spine.

His wife was near death when I reached her. There was nothing we could have done, even if I'd had adequate supplies. Her body was emaciated beyond belief, more skeleton than flesh. Her eyes were so wide, Jean. I cannot imagine the pain she experienced in those last moments. Her final breath was barely a wheeze.

I assisted in the burial alongside the husband and local gravedigger. I was unsure what else to do. A crowd—news travels fast here, evidently—had gathered, but kept their distance until I left the cemetery. Then, a local approached me demanding assistance.

"You're a Doctor," he exclaimed. "Surely you have some remedy, a tonic to cure us!" His desperation was palpable.

A portly woman then tugged at my sleeve—she had lost two daughters. "The demon took my babies," she sobbed.

I inquired if they had a local doctor, only to be informed he, too, had died. More gathered around me, pointing fingers, some crying. I could scarcely refuse to help. I admit, I was quite curious, and the thought of myself or the crew becoming sick, for whatever reason, never crossed my mind. We've been through so much, I expect I've been slightly desensitised to death and disease. I promised the crowd I'd look into it and told them where to find me if they had other patients.

They hope I can solve this … conundrum. Once again, I seem to be the best option—the only option—for medical intervention. However, the likelihood of success, from where I stand right now, is infinitesimally small. Wyatt consulted Deborah who said, "The path is clouded," whatever that means. He and the others attending to the Goddess are kept occupied making sure She doesn't dry out. Wyatt explained this is the first time they'd been landlocked for many moons, and the discomfort She felt echoed through the crew.

George found me as I was making my way back to the crew's nest, warning me, "Now that the Devil has taken my sweet Dorabelle, there's no telling who it's passed on to. It could be one of you lot. You should watch your back, Doctor."

Filled with dread, no doubt accentuated by our quasi-marooned conditions, I studied every person I encountered that night for signs others had missed. I spent all night trying to think of a solution to this problem and realised I had to collect more information about this creature. The more you know about an animal, the easier it is to understand its habitat, behaviours, and weaknesses, right, Jean?

On the second day, I was beset by visitors, townsfolk who had known someone afflicted by the Skin Dweller and were desperate to share whatever information they could in case it helped. Here are my findings:

Firstly, I do not believe this Skin Dweller is a demon. Everything has a scientific answer. Equating the unknown to the underworld is human nature, but you and I are scientists.

The Skin Dweller appears to be a parasitic organism that exclusively lives and feeds on human hosts. In all cases, the host expires within a few days, sometimes mere hours after the parasite leaves their body. Unfortunately, villagers bury victims immediately and will not let me perform autopsies. This practice was something their priest suggested before his untimely end—he was one of the first victims. An understandable measure, but unhelpful to my efforts.

I'll need to figure out a way to test who's been infected. And quickly.

There's so much I wish to tell you, but I need to run to the docks if I have any hope of making it there before the ships leave. Praying to the Gods, both large and small, to protect me and get me through this.

WB

P.S. It seems my verbosity has cursed me once again. The port authority at Tortuga has closed off the bay. I suppose I'll keep these letters with me and mark them for your care in case the worst happens.

I have to wonder, did you ever receive my other letters? Did you read them?

Will I ever hear from you again?

August 30th, 1760

ENTRY FROM JEAN BAPTISTE DE BEAUPRÉ'S JOURNAL

FROM WILLIE'S LETTERS, I had half assumed that life at sea would be one of chaos and bloodshed. However, it was a rather quiet ride until today.

The lack of excitement has not helped with my propensity to worry about Wilford. The crew has been keeping me busy with some menial work; they seem happy that I'm not some whining upper-class good-for-nothing passenger. I mended sails and swept the decks for the first couple of days until I got to chatting with the Doctor/Chef about my studies of the Natural Sciences over dinner. Since then, he's enlisted my help with some doctoring and with his experiments to create a self-sustaining garden for fresh food on the long voyages.

Yesterday, we discovered some rather enterprising algae had contaminated our water supply, and while we could still use it to safely water our plants, drinking it would poison the crew. Luckily (or due to the Tear's intervention), we weren't far from an island with freshwater springs, so we shifted our course.

This morning, I was gently awoken by a tapping on my door.

Apparently, I was going to be joining the offshore party since "The Tear saw you as part of the team."

I'll be honest, I'd heard enough stories of wild animals and dangerous islands from Willie to feel some trepidation as we rowed closer. But since he managed to survive for months at sea, I could too. And the Tear would be unlikely to send me to my doom this early in our journey. It was only later that I remembered the crew had said they don't always get Their prophecies right.

The island was a green expanse more sprawling than Oxford. Colourful birds flew over the verdant canopy, their distant calls audible from the rowboat. It would have seemed paradisiacal; however, I knew better than to be lulled into a sense of security.

"Stay on the path," Da'mon said as we all disembarked.

The perfectly white sand let out a plaintive whine with every step we took, like the wailing of long-lost sailors warning us to stay away. But none of the crew paid it any mind—I later learned it was a natural phenomenon due to the properties of the sand—and I charged after them and into the forest.

At first, I could not see the winding "path" and simply tried to step in the boot prints of the man ahead of me. Gradually, I began to note where the brush had been slightly cleared, vines cut away by those who had come before us.

I was carefully watching where I was placing my feet when I saw something white reaching out of the brush like a rib-like fern. I bent down and noticed it was not some strange plant but a skeletal hand, inches from where I was about to place my foot.

I am not proud of the scream I let out, nor of the fact that I point-edly did not listen to Da'mon's instructions. I went careening off the path and into the dense vegetation, away from the hand and directly back to the beach. I could actually smell the green frustration of the plants I crushed underfoot. The crew implored me to return, but a primal need to flee death possessed me.

In retrospect, I put myself in much greater danger than what I would have faced on the trail.

By the time a hand grabbed my shoulder and stopped me, toppling me onto my ass, I had dived deep into the thick vine-covered understory. As I struggled to find my breath and untangle myself from the thick frond carpet, the rest of the crew caught up. Da'mon helped me to my feet as one of the crew gasped, pointing ahead.

Dangling from a vine several metres ahead of us was a gleaming, gem-encrusted dagger. Likely worth a small fortune, it was a very tempting lure for any pirate.

"Is that …?" a deckhand asked.

I do not know this crew as well as Wil does his and mostly refer to them by their assignments.

"I never thought I'd see it again!" the boatswain said.

"It's more beautiful than I remembered!" another deckhand said.

"Well, at least we know where it got off to," Da'mon mused.

The dagger had once belonged to the Captain, who had lost it in a wager—the details of which I was not privy to, but their silence led me to believe it had been particularly humiliating.

"I bet the Captain would excuse whoever brought that back from privy duties for a month!" the first deckhand exclaimed, sending all three men into a mad scramble through the vines, tripping over one another to claim the prize.

It was then I noticed that the vine holding the knife was different from the ones at our feet. Instead of green, it was dark red and covered in fine spines. It was dangling the dagger over a suspiciously round puddle several feet in diameter, surrounded by a lip the same colour as the vine.

It was a trap!

I called out to the trio, but the second deckhand was already leaping up to grab the dagger. When he fell into the water patch below, his feet sizzled and steamed like meat on a fire. He continued to sink past his ankles, his knees. It was much deeper than a puddle.

He screamed as the bubbling liquid covered his head, drowning him. I'm certain it only lasted a few moments, but in my mind it went on forever. Skin bursting like geysers, revealing the angry red muscle underneath as he desperately flailed his arms. Soon his cries turned to gagging as the stream reached his throat, clogging his airway. I tried to look away, but it was as if I was frozen to the spot. The two others scrambled towards him, but a large leaf slammed over the hole like the lid over a mug of ale, sealing the contents within.

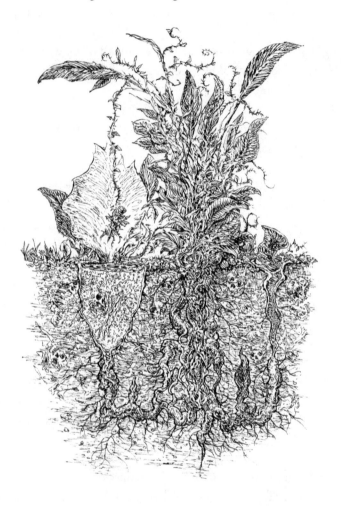

Da'mon brought out his cutlass, slicing the thick leaf several times before he managed to cut all the way through. Together, we peeled open the leaf as he stuck his hand (the one without the tattoo) into the murky, reeking brown liquid I later learned was the acidic digestive juices of a gigantic carnivorous plant native to the area. He groaned as his skin sizzled and bubbled. We grabbed onto him, lending him our strength to pull out the deckhand. The poor fellow emerged with a scream, his skin red and bubbling, covered in pus-filled blisters. The crew wiped off what they could of the sticky, foul-smelling goo with leaves. A too-strong wipe pulled off a flap from his cheek. We carried him back to the beach. It was only then that we noticed that he was still clutching the dagger.

"That is why we stick to the path," Da'mon told me as we rowed the deckhand back to the Doctor before setting back into the forest to complete our mission. This time I noticed more of them, the treasure lures. There were necklaces coated in gems, an ancient helm, some daggers, and a shining gun I had no doubt would have lured Barlowe to a watery doom. A handful were visible from the path, which winded away from the temptation of the glints and gleams of treasure.

We made several trips to fill up all our barrels, and that night, my muscles ached as much as Wilford's had after sword practice.

Perhaps this connection will allow me to see him better tonight.

In my sleep, I see flashes of Willie, and I'm not sure if these are meant to be visions from the Tear or simply dreams. Am I ready to entertain the idea that this creature on the topmast is even capable of such a thing as precognition? I'm not sure. But I suppose little else can explain the fact that They knew so much about Willie and me. It might be time I let go of the scientific rigidity I have always worn as a cloak. I am simply not in Oxford anymore.

September 2nd, 1760

ENTRY FROM JEAN BAPTISTE DE BEAUPRÉ'S JOURNAL

I AWOKE LONG after dawn's breaking to a cacophony of voices, then a boom so loud and forceful it rattled my core. After catching my breath, I realised I could hear it—singing, if that's what you could call the strange strident howls of the sirens Wilford described in his letters. The one creature he faced where he'd found no clever way to save himself and the crew, they'd only gotten away through the sacrifice of one of their number. I couldn't fathom sharing this information with my crew: how would we choose which individual to sacrifice for the good of the many? A wave of panic overcame me and I scrambled into my coat before heading above deck with my hands covering my ears … only to be greeted by the entire crew happily working as if nothing was amiss. Thankfully, no one was looking in my direction. I'm sure my cheeks were flush with embarrassment.

A deckhand named Percy lit a small powder flask before tossing it in the water where it landed in the middle of a large school of fish. A moment later, another BOOM shook the ship and a cheer rose up among the crew. Fish, resembling those Willie described, flew into the air, some landing on the deck while others plopped back into the sea. A few held long poles that descended into the waters while others held a large net by its edges, gathering the stragglers.

"Monsieur Jean! You're awake!" Da'mon greeted me with a laugh, put a hand on my shoulder, not unkindly, and steered me towards the port side where most of the crew were gathered.

"What's going on?"

"Ah, we are gathering the choir—they're needed where we're going." As he spoke, the noise grew weaker but maintained a steady tone. I still felt nervous, but there appeared to be no danger presently. With each explosion, the singing quieted.

"Choir? Do you mean these… fish?"

From up close, their scales had an undeniable resemblance to pruned skin. They looked like a person who had been in the bath for too long. Their faces, too, were uncanny, almost humanlike in appearance. Their bruise-purple, prominent lips flapped open and closed while their gills fluttered uselessly. Outside the water, they were unable to produce their strident song but resumed afresh when placed in crowded barrels that covered the deck. Crew wrapped the barrels in sails to deaden the sound (the same solution Wilford had proposed!) before bringing them to the hold. He would have been thrilled about the research possibilities, but I was more interested in the culinary aspects. It was enough food to feed us for weeks! I'd grown tired of the vegetable patch on deck and was ready for some meat. I'd just hope the heads didn't still look as human once they hit my plate.

Another blast went off, making Da'mon yell to be heard. "I can see you thinking, my friend! They're not for us. Taste pretty bad to people—like old boots doused in horse piss! But they're a delicacy for the Flock."

They've started to predict my questions before I ask them! Is this another trick of the Tear, or am I really that obvious?

The singing continued to diminish as more and more fish landed on the deck. What was once a full orchestra had become little more than a carolling choir. The remaining fish, grasping the danger, dispersed back into the deep. Gulls swooped in to pick the scraps littering the sea foam.

I glanced back up at the Tear, forever watching. The attendant for the day had covered the top of the cage with a sail to protect the sensitive creature from the sun's rays. I was touched by this simple act of kindness, even towards something so grotesque.

I admit these pirates are quite unlike the bloodthirsty ruffians I've read about, nor are they like the chaotic mess Willie found himself saddled with. I'm beginning to think this will work out after all.

Hold on, Wil. I'll be there soon.

September 3rd, 1760

ENTRY FROM JEAN BAPTISTE DE BEAUPRÉ'S JOURNAL

I HAD THE QUEEREST DREAM. Even now, the pictures blur and fade, so I must hurry to write it all down before it is lost.

I saw Wilford surrounded by bodies that seemed hollow, like skins prepped for taxidermy before being stuffed. Despite their lack of bones and muscles, the skins moved as if animated by the wind. Wilford tried to evade their grasping hands and gaping toothless mouths, but the strange creatures blocked his every step.

There was more: I saw flashes of black snakes falling from eye sockets, Wil's face covered in dark, congealed blood and streaked tears, and a grinning thing that looked like an infant wrapped in a moth's cocoon. I could not understand what I was seeing, other than the fact that Wil is in grave peril, which the Tear had already indicated. Perhaps it was the Tear that also gave me these visions? I will see if I can find Da'mon, if he's had similar experiences.

As suspected, Da'mon says the dream is likely a gift from the Tear. While I find myself disturbed by Their ability to so easily enter my mind, and the terror of the images They've shown me, I'm also happy to have seen Wilford again, to know he is still alive. I beg the winds to pick up and push us faster along our journey.

With the rising dawn, I also discovered a strange patch of raised skin on my hand where all the others have their eye tattoos. My body marked by the voyage, I am less and less likely to be able to return to any semblance of normal life once this ordeal is done. But what am I missing really, other than Wilford? Books, fine dining? That doesn't seem like much. I had always been so paralysed by fear, picturing every worst-case scenario and unable to act in case one of them came true. I could not go back to that kind of life.

Besides, I disliked being surrounded by reminders of Wil's absence. At least at sea, I am not constantly barraged by memories of him. At least here, I feel like I am doing something productive, something that will help him.

I blow into the sails whenever I pass by.

September 3rd, 1760

LETTER FROM WILFORD BOWEN TO JEAN BAPTISTE DE BEAUPRÉ

Dear Jean,

Things have gotten worse since my last letter. And not just for the crew. The Goddess sits in a corner of the warehouse den, pale and deflated. Her once vibrant skin is mottled, the fresh barrels of seawater offering no nourishment. No one wants to speak it aloud, but if we don't get back to the ocean soon … She will surely perish. A sadness radiates through our den, and I find it hard to be in close proximity to Her.

While I have made inroads on the mystery of the Skin Dweller, I do not yet nearly have enough to guarantee our safety. Firstly, everyone in the village now travels in groups. The affliction seems to strike when a person is alone and thus vulnerable, although it will also wipe out entire households in the course of an evening. Of course, someone was bound to fall victim eventually. Luckily—which feels rotten to say under the circumstances—I found the corpse. We wrapped it in cloth and quietly moved it to our temporary lodging for an autopsy. Tommy assisted (well, he stood beside me and grimaced).

It was a young man, Samuel Porter, perhaps twenty years of age (his parents were no longer with us, so this was my best approximation). As with Dorabelle, Samuel's body was gaunt, with nearly all muscle tissue degraded. His veins still contained blood; however, it was as thick as syrup. I inspected every inch of him, which while enlightening, was dour.

It was a long, arduous process (my tools were rudimentary at best), but after several hours, I finally discovered a clue.

I noticed a very slight discoloration, a purplish bruise, on the right tear duct. I peeled back the eyelids and noticed some dark webbing, somewhat similar to the pattern of veins under the skin but above rather than below the flesh. To Tommy's consternation, I removed the eye and found a webbed material not unlike that which a spider produces, branching until it entered the optic nerve hole in the skull. It was black as night until this point, then gradually lightening (I'm assuming) as it mixed with Samuel's blood. Was this where the creature entered? Did it undergo some sort of metamorphosis once inside? If it entered through such a small hole, the creature itself was likely miniscule, or capable of changing its form, such as an octopus that could fit through a hole the size of its beak.

I'm unsure if the discoloration was from the creature's entry or exit. In addition, the discoloration alone might not be enough of a sign of infection; four out of the five crew members had similar discoloration, probably due to lack of sleep and worry over the Goddess. However, I do believe that removal of the eye might be a good way to evaluate whether the Skin Dweller has infected a host.

Due to its rather permanent consequences, this extreme measure should only be taken if one had rather convincing evidence of an individual's possession.

I told Tommy to find Captain Samson, and he sprinted off without hesitation.

I followed his example and went to the tavern to announce my discovery, only to be stopped by Wyatt. He put a hand on my shoulder and said with resignation, unsurprised that he'd lost yet another loved one, "It got Lindsay."

It really did hit me then, the danger we were in.

And this death, it was my fault.

If I had been quicker, I could have saved him, Jean.

We gathered around his body, which Mac was quickly wrapping in cloth. His arm, dried and covered in flies disappeared behind a white sheet—he'd likely died that morning, perhaps before Samuel. I was glad I didn't need to do an autopsy. I don't think I could stomach seeing more of his corpse. I wanted to remember him as he was. His belly laugh and the way he always found the bright side of any bad situation. I'd quite liked Lindsay, and I saw quite a bit of him in my clinic, what with his propensity to injury (often to save his crewmates from an even worse fate). I'd started thinking he was somehow immune to death, having dodged it so many times. It was foolish, I realise that now, Jean, but it had been a comfort to think of him this way.

Mac led the crew in song, and then men bowed their heads. Although Mac was close to Lindsay, his voice never broke. I looked up and saw he was looking back at me, a tear rolling down his cheek.

"You understand the gravity of the situation… we're all at risk. Even the Goddess." I had never seen Barlowe this frustrated. Even his tattoos appeared affected, their once bright ink now dull against his skin. They no longer move, no matter how hard he tries to coax them back to life. The Goddess simply does not have the power to sustain them. He's shaken off any attempt I've made to help, saying, "The Goddess's mystery is much greater than anything your scientific method can comprehend. There's nothing you or medicine can do."

He'd never been this sharp with me before. It's clear the Goddess means a great deal more to him than I ever could.

Tommy had dragged Captain Samson back to the pub when we arrived, still solemn from the funeral. Everyone was relieved to see him until he refused to tell us where he had been. "Captain's business," he kept repeating.

"I know where he's been," Tommy piped up from behind me. "I found him with a woman."

As soon as the words left his mouth, the crew was yelling. A cry of "Blasphemer!" went up, and I could see this feeling was mutual among those present.

Loyal in mind and flesh.

"Listen! She's the local witch. I've been requesting her help with the Goddess, to make Her time on land less painful." Despite this explanation, the Captain looked uncomfortable. "I know it's forbidden to get outsiders involved… but what choice do I have?"

"How *dare* you," Barlowe was spitting rage, his finger jabbing squarely on the Captain's chest, pushing him back. "She honours us with Her gifts, protects us, and when She's near death, you betray Her?"

Like a cornered animal, the Captain puffed up to his full height. Gone was the hesitation and discomfort of moments ago.

"She chose *me*, not you. I know what is best for Her. And you question that judgement?"

I tried to get between the two of them, but it was too late.

Barlowe was a man possessed, his love for the Goddess blinding him. He smashed his fist into the Captain's face and continued beating him as he crumpled to the ground. It took three men to pull him off.

Wyatt stepped in and helped a bloodied Captain Samson to his feet. "Lock him up for now. The crew will decide what to do with him."

The rest of the evening was tense.

Everyone is so close to blows that it's hard to know if they'll finish each other off before the Skin Dweller has a chance.

There have been no deaths to my knowledge since Samuel's, which is a blessing, but with each passing hour, unrest rises. We have no way of tracking who it will take next.

I'm worried what will happen when this comes to a boil.

-W

September 5th, 1760

ENTRY FROM JEAN BAPTISTE DE BEAUPRÉ'S JOURNAL

I'M NOT sure how Wilford deals with this. Every single day, something fantastical or horrific happens—sometimes in equal measure. I feel run ragged, yet we cannot stop.

The crew is guided by some internal logic—or guidance from the Tear—I am not completely party to yet, although I get glimpses of a pattern within my dreams. I find these hints of our future assuage the fears that used to plague me in England. Perhaps it's the influence from the creature on the mast, or the closing distance between myself and Wil that calms me. Perhaps both.

Either way, after catching the fish, our next destination was an island with steep white cliffs bordering three sides, and a small crescent-shaped bay. I was shocked to see the small island had a dock! The crew tied up the ship and began unloading the barrels of fish. Captain Tiberius led the crew up the steep island path, all of us participating in the Sisyphean task of pushing these barrels uphill. Arms burning and legs shaking, we eventually crested the top and reached a plateau upon which rested a colony of dozens of giant birds!

I had seen some seabirds on our journey that made the gulls on the cliffs of Dover look like garden robins: pelicans with their throats bulging with fish; frigate birds that seemed to soar endlessly on hidden currents; albatross with wings that stretched longer than three metres! All of those were unimpressive compared to the Flock.

The birds' heads towered over our own. One flapped wings nearly half the width of our boat in a threat display.

They looked almost reptilian, long beaks tipped with sharp hooks. Their dark eyes were non-reflective pits into which light travelled, never to emerge. One broke away from the group to take a closer look at us. Their confident stride and movement spoke of its cunning, its determination. I did not want it to see me as dinner, I felt I was unlikely to come out of that experience whole.

Its plumage was dark with an iridescent shimmer that bent the light around it like the inverse of a rainbow. The head on its long neck swivelled, taking us in before tilting up as it issued a strident call. I covered my ears while the *Watchman*'s crew simply flinched. This was not their first time visiting the island.

Tiberius pried off the top of a barrel, unleashing the tearful wailing of the Choir fish. It sounded all too much like the crying of babes.

There was a mad cacophony of squawks as the Flock descended upon the cask, smashing it with their beaks and catching the squirming fish as they flopped in muddy puddles. Their wings generated winds that blew from every direction and nearly knocked me down the steep mountain path. I threw myself down on the earth, covering my head to dodge their sharp talons. The crew hurriedly pried open the other barrels as if afraid they'd be next on the menu. The whole ordeal lasted a couple of minutes, after which the birds peeled off in pairs to groom, a handful remaining with us.

The Captain walked up to one, placing his tattooed hand on the bowed head of the largest of the group with a gnarly crack in its beak and a featherless, scarred patch the size of a plate close to its heart.

I looked over at Da'mon for an explanation, but he was staring in reverence at the silent exchange. We stood for much longer than the birds took to devour their meal, but eventually, the leader stood back, calling stridently six times. A couple of the larger birds clambered back over.

"We'll have the assistance of the Flock," Tiberius said, which prompted a joyous outcry from the crew. The birds took off, the scarred leader returning to his roost while we picked our way down the steep path. By the time we arrived at the dock, those who had remained on the ship had nearly finished strapping leather harnesses to those of the Flock who would accompany us on our journey. The birds patiently bobbed in the waves as we climbed onboard.

When the ropes that secured us to the dock were untied, the Captain pulled out a shell and blew several times, the sounds imitating the cries of the birds. They flapped up from the waves, beads of water falling on us and catching the sunlight to create a more hopeful rainbow than the ones their feathers emitted.

The birds took off, jerking the boat forward. I grasped the mast, lest I be knocked over again. The Captain stood at the prow, calling up directions while we sped along much faster than we could even with sails pregnant with a strong wind. Our boat created a white turbulent wake.

"Shouldn't be too long now," Da'mon told me.

I hoped so. It had already been long enough.

September 8th, 1760

ENTRY FROM JEAN BAPTISTE DE BEAUPRÉ'S JOURNAL

THE FLOCK MADE the journey in the blink of an eye.

Three ships branded as Tortuga Port Authority formed a chain across the bay, barricading the port. We sent over a rowboat to the lead ship and waited as the Tear relayed the conversation. The Port Authority maintained that the island was infested with "a monster that wears the flesh of its victims"—I hoped this was a mistranslation. Our pleas to be let through, that we were there to help were ignored for "our own safety." The Captain climbed up to the crow's nest and talked to the Tear to gather "information that could help." He came back down with a smirk, saying the emissary had been sent a vision he could use to blackmail the Port Authority's Director to let us through. After a couple of agonising minutes, the Port Authority boats shifted their barrage to grant us passage. We untied the birds, per Port Authority commands; we didn't need them any longer.

"We're not getting back out unless we neutralise the threat," Tiberius told me as he leapt down onto the deck. I swore to him I would do that and more.

I'm unsure from where my sudden conviction arose, but it felt right.

Our ship had scarcely pulled into port before I climbed down the ropes and ran into town. I could hear Da'mon shouting after me to wait, but I didn't care. Wil was here, I knew it. I had begun to trust the Tear's predictions and connect the dots. They didn't—or couldn't—tell you exactly how things would occur—but They gave you enough foresight to reach the next step, and from there the path would be clear.

The town looked abandoned, empty streets and shut windows, locked doors. An overturned barrel blocked a street while a mangy dog chewing what looked like a human tibia growled at me as I approached. I saw no townsfolk as I journeyed from port and into the streets. I hoped the residents of Tortuga were barricaded indoors, still alive, protected and not entombed. That we had not come too late. That the monster had not already decimated the town while the Port Authority tanned and gambled on their decks.

The silence of the town was uncomfortable. After weeks at sea, I'd grown used to the constant chatter of the crew, the creaking of the ship, the rush of waves, the crying of gulls. Now I was truly alone, no crew, no Willie.

I came to an inn and tavern—the Boot and Heel—its door thrown wide open. Empty.

A chair had been overturned, but otherwise, the place looked untouched, as if everyone had simply vanished. The casks behind the bar were all intact (I'd figured they'd been the first things to be taken or smashed by looters), a rag was bunched on the counter. The hearth had grown cold, and the cauldron that hung over a pile of ashes smelled rank, the food in it gone bad.

"Wilford?" I tried.

No one answered but my echo.

I kept walking, seeing movement, only to turn the corner and discover a leaf flying in the wind or a rat scurrying to safety. I was far enough from the sea to no longer hear or smell it, which was oddly disquieting. But in its absence, I could make out shouting ahead. I followed it, backtracking more than once in the winding, dead-end streets until I came to the market square.

It was packed with hundreds of people squeezed into the tight space, likely all the remaining living residents of the town. Over-turned carts littered the street, sagging under the weight of multiple people trying to get a better view. Amongst the screams, I made out the plea: "Kill him! Kill him!" The crowd pressed me on all sides. I panicked, afraid of being crushed, afraid that Wilford was the one whose death they were cheering for. I pushed forward, knowing—sensing—that he was at the centre of this and desperate to get to him. But the crowd was just too dense, too furious to let me through. Brute force wouldn't work against this village of fishermen and labourers, at least not the force I was capable of.

I climbed onto a nearby cart. Finally, I could see to the centre of the square where a circle of men stood, eyes filled with murderous intent, blades drawn on a man whose face was beaten black and blue, whose white-blond hair was streaked with blood. It wasn't Wilford.

Someone climbed up on the dais with the other men. He was facing away from me, but I knew the back of that head, the weight of his step.

My stomach flipped, my legs moved of their own accord. I nearly fell off the cart.

"Wilford!" I called to him.

He turned, the glorious head I never thought I'd see again, the same Wilford I'd known for years. But he was different; he held himself taller now, more confident and sure of himself.

The smile that broke out on his face upon seeing me nearly made me weep.

I'd have run to him then, but the wall of townsfolk stood as a barricade between us.

"Jean?" His voice. Oh his voice! He sounded so happy to see me, breaking on the question.

A stream of bloody tears leaked down from the haggard man's face—the Captain, I later learned—where Wilford pressed a blade.

A large-chested man with tattoos stood close, much too close, to Willie—that must have been Barlowe. The entire bunch looked exhausted, their shoulders slumped and sweat-soaked hair plastered to their foreheads.

My right hand began to shake. I reached out to still it, but it was as impossible to stop as an earthquake. My elbow bent as my hand rose of its own volition, stilling only once it covered my right eye. My vision was dark until, like the opening of an eye, an aperture formed on my hand. Wisps of brilliant colour overtook my vision, each person bathed in light, as if their very souls had become visible— except one boy standing just behind the Captain. His were a tangled mess of black, enveloping his body like a ball of yarn, or like the threads of a moth weaving its cocoon. For a split second, I was over- come with a heavy wave of disgust, like the time I'd accidentally split a cocoon only to find the innards full of goo. I blinked and regained control over my hand, pushing it down.

My dream.

"The boy!" I yelled. "The black snakes are in the boy!"

Wil's eyebrows furrowed for a moment before they shot up, and he spun around. "Tommy? But ... when? How?"

Tommy, or the thing that wore Tommy, raised his palms defen- sively and cried, "No! You know me, Sir. I'm just who I say I am. He's the Dweller, must be, to arrive at a time like this!"

"I can see the blackness within him," I told everyone, but Wil especially. In crept my old fears: that I had let him go, that he had such life-altering experiences with this crew, that I had gotten the Fellowship he deserved, had irreparably damaged our bond. His trust in me. That, after all this time, all those adventures they'd shared, he would side with his crew.

I brought my hand to my face once more, willing the eye to open. I was proud that this was something I could now control, that I wouldn't just be the Tear's puppet. But what really hit me was the look of joy, of unflinching belief I saw in Wil's face. I had not lost this battle.

"Damn you," Tommy spat. "Getting help from Gods, that's

playing dirty." His face twitched, a black worm slithering under his eye and down to his neck and then disappearing. A tentacle sprung from his wrist, and he waved it wildly, nearly hitting Wilford, who let out a cry.

A shout of "It's him! The demon!" rose from the crowd. Everyone took a worried step back, afraid it would invade whoever it landed on.

The boy fell to the ground, gouging his nails along his face, rupturing his own eyes. The creature burst through the wounds and slithered across the cobbles, twisting through the cracks between the stones, leaving behind the shrivelled body of the cabin boy. Black tendrils spread like the roots of a tree, branching toward each individual. A man slashed his blade at the ground, cutting the threads clean. The lines shrunk back momentarily before continuing their approach.

A screech broke through the shouts.

An older, bearded man was pulled down, threads wrapping around his legs and up his groin. The searching black roots along the ground receded, everything pulling into the new target. The old man's eyes grew wide and sweat ran down his forehead.

"Shoot me!" he waved his arms frantically before the black threads entangled them and pinned him down. Tendrils streaked his face, heading towards his tear ducts. He convulsed as the creature infiltrated his body.

A shot rang out, red bloomed between his eyes. The silence that followed was broken only by the ringing in my ears.

His body quivered for a moment before being forcibly inverted, the head and chest sucked into his belly with an audible crunch, the flesh turning in on itself, a rain of blood falling into the street like water from a wrung mop. Wet tendrils whipped out of the muscle, fat, and bone mass like a poisoned anemone, and everyone scrambled back, fearful that it was trying to find another victim.

But the tendrils did not search for another. Instead they wrapped around the central mass, expanding it. It kept growing, pulsing, coal-dark lustrous tendrils, piling up on top of one another, slithering around and around like a sentient, monstrous ball of yarn until it was as big as a fully grown man. Then it fell completely still. The street was eerily quiet but for the plink of the lead shot the creature ejected onto the cobbles. Someone threw a rock that rebounded softly off the black mass, but it was still, unharmed.

Not dead; waiting. Transitioning to its final form.

I brought my new eye up to look at the creature. It blinked open, and I saw—inside the mass was a soft jelly.

My mind flashed to my studies, my work—the moths.

The beast was cocooning itself, preparing for the next phase of life. I couldn't let that happen.

"For God's sake," I cried to them. "Cut it open!"

Barlowe's blade flashed, and the skin burst open, splashing foul tar upon the ground and my shoes. The stench of sewage was overwhelming, and I covered my face with a sleeve to keep from gagging. Acrid rot stinging my eyes, I watched the mass bubble like stew left too long in the pot, thick and sticky. I could see the aborted beginnings of limbs, sinuous half-formed fingers, things I couldn't identify that would never come to fruition. A high-pitched squeal erupted from the beast, and a lone tendril crawled from a newly opened orifice, dragging the sac toward the closest man.

I saw a shape in the corner of my eye and turned to see their Captain, back on his feet. He calmly lit a match and brought it to the pipe between his lips, taking a long drag.

After a long exhale of smoke, he flicked the match directly into the writhing, black mass. For something so wet, it caught flame instantly like an oil-soaked rag. An audible whoosh accompanied the warm blast as the creature squirmed but had no mouth with which to scream. The flames were a deep blue, and a rotten smell filled my nostrils and burned my eyes as thick dark smoke filled the square.

"Goddess be with you," Captain Samson said.

We stood in silence as it stilled and burned to ash. I caught my breath and looked around. I felt a strange sense of familiarity. This was the crew my Wil had shared all his waking hours with for months, making me green with envy.

Wilford stood a few feet away, clearly dazed. I finally took in his full appearance; tanned, strong. Several days of stubble covered his

cheeks, making him appear years older, not months. More in possession of himself than in a frantic need to gain everyone's approval.

A flood of emotions overtook me then. I crossed the distance to
Wil and embraced him, tears welling up as I buried my face into his
chest, taking in his familiar scent even under the months of salt air. I
had so much I wanted to tell him, but when I pulled back—he spoke
first.

"How did you find me? Did you get my letters? But... I didn't
even send the ones from Tortuga. Wait... you're not mad at me for
leaving?" His eyes met mine briefly before looking away, ashamed.

"Of course I'm not mad!" I was shocked he would even think it!
"As for how I got here—that's quite the story. One to rival your own,
I expect."

"I'm... relieved you're here." His body leaned towards mine as if
he experienced the same magnetic pull I did towards him. "I missed
you."

Something broke in me then. "Oh, fuck it."

I kissed him.

All of my fears washed away when, a moment later, he took my
face in his hands and kissed me back. I couldn't help but let out a
laugh, and he joined in, wiping the tears that fell from my eyes. I
leaned into his touch, relishing the closeness I had craved for so long.

It was better than my wildest dreams.

"The Goddess was right; I needed to listen to my heart," he said.

"What do you mean?" I asked him.

"Jean... I was scared—that I wasn't good enough for you, that I
would never be. Especially after my rejection from the Royal Society... I felt like I needed to show you I was capable of more."

"We've both been fools. I should have never let you run away like
that," I said.

"And I should have brought you with me."

"From now on, I'll go where you go."

What followed was rather tawdry and will remain between the
two of us rather than written where prying eyes might see. Wilford
did get a lot of grins and back slaps when we sat down for breakfast
the next day, which makes me think that even without a written

record, the crew were able to paint quite their own picture. Barlowe gave me a deep nod from his place beside the battered Captain, who was in surprisingly good spirits, considering.

Wil's never been a quiet one. But he seems happy and grins as he reads over my shoulder. That's all that really matters, isn't it, Wil?

Of course I am happy, my love.

September 23rd, 1760

LETTER FROM JEAN BAPTISTE DE BEAUPRÉ TO NELKA MAZUR, AT CANDLELIGHT PUBLICATIONS

To the most esteemed Nelka Mazur,

Please find attached a collection of letters and journal entries detailing the findings from Wilford Bowen's (and mine, I suppose) maritime adventures. While the contents of this bundle of pages may seem fantastical, if not impossible, to you, I assure you every page captures our observations to the best of our linguistic ability. *Nullum magnum ingenium sine mixtura dementiae fuit* — There has been no great wisdom without an element of madness.

One day, the secrets of the seas will find their way back to land, and Wilford Bowen's letters will be known as artefacts of great scientific value. And to think of the importance — the esteem! — of the brilliant individual who chose to publish these tales! I'd hate for it to be anyone other than you.

In the meantime, it's up to you to decide if they should be sold as fiction or truth. Wilford Bowen and I will continue our travels and discoveries — together. I know what happens to men like us back in

England, or France, for that matter. You'd be surprised how little judgement there is on the high seas.

Over the last few weeks, I've felt happier than I've been in years. I no longer go about my day with an ache in my breast. Can you imagine that? More comfortable among pirates and thieves, murderers and vagrants than my Oxford colleagues or my Royal Society Fellows? My research holds no candle to this adventure. Moths feel altogether trivial when you've seen a God. Rather, *Gods*. Plural!

We've been tasked with overseeing the Goddess and her health by Captain Samson. The men have their own way of appeasing Her —but for myself and Willie, the scientific side of things is far more interesting. The joy of discovery and study is all I require to be happy. That, and my Wil.

-Jean Baptiste de Beaupré

Acknowledgments

A ship cannot reach its destination with only its co-captains onboard, so Lor and Shelley would like to thank the following crew:

Their keen-eyed betas standing at top of the mast and steering them to clear waters: Steve Neal and Alexis Dubon.

Their wise and precise editor Eric Raglin, for keeping the ship on course.

Their sponsor and treasurer, Nelka Mazur at Hedone Books, for greenlighting the voyage.

Their village criers and early blurbers, spreading the word of the book: Joe Koch, J.A.W. McCarthy, Emett Nahil, Dori Lumpkin, Tiffany Michelle Brown, Caitlin Marceau, Sapphire Lazuli.

Their seer, Kyle, who always had new paths forward when stuck on a sandbar.

Their friends and family, the seven seas couldn't begin to encompass our gratitude.

Last but certainly not least: the ship's cats, Bean, Beeb, and Pierogi, who kept the ship free of mice and laps covered in hair.

About the Authors

SHELLEY LAVIGNE is a purveyor of moist literature, usually queer horror. They live in Ontario, Canada and use their science degrees for unintended purposes, including writing this novella. Their words can be found in various places including but not limited to *The Dread Machine*, *If There's Anyone Left* and in collaboration with Eric Raglin and Lor Gislason in *Sick! Stories from the Goop Troop* (Ghoulish Books). You can also find them online at shelleylavigne.com

LOR GISLASON is a non-binary homebody from Vancouver Island, Canada who explores horror through an autistic lens and has been featured in various anthologies including *Re:Wired*, *Hear Us Scream*, *Ooze* and *Escalators from Hell*. They are the editor of *Bound in Flesh: An Anthology of Trans Body Horror*. For more info visit lormaggot.ca

Detailed Content Warnings

Gore/Violence
Trypophobia
Bugs
Character/animal death
Homophobia
The callous way scientists view death
Sexual content

Printed in the USA
CPSIA information can be obtained
at www.ICGtesting.com
CBHW072330080824
12905CB00050B/1283